BOOK 3

THE KITTEN WHO SCARED A GHOST

NOVA DUBOIS

Printed in the United States of America
Hardcover ISBN: 978-1-959096-25-2
Paperback ISBN: 978-1-959096-26-9
Ebook ISBN: 978-1-959096-27-6

Library of Congress Control Number: 2022947167

Canoe Tree Press

4697 Main Street
Manchester Center, VT 05255
Canoe Tree Press is a division of DartFrog Books

vinestreetmysteries.com

To Terri - whose strength, perseverance,
and tenacity are role models for us all.

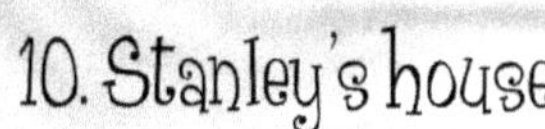

10. Stanley's house

9. Makawee Public Library

Legend:
1. Pearl's house
2. Little Paws Clinic
3. Pearly White Dentistry
4. Sweet Georgina's Chocolate Shoppe
5. Pebbles' House
6. Makawee Elementary
7. Mr. Steve's House

8
MAKAWEE HOSPITAL
8. Makawee Hospital
4
2
9
3

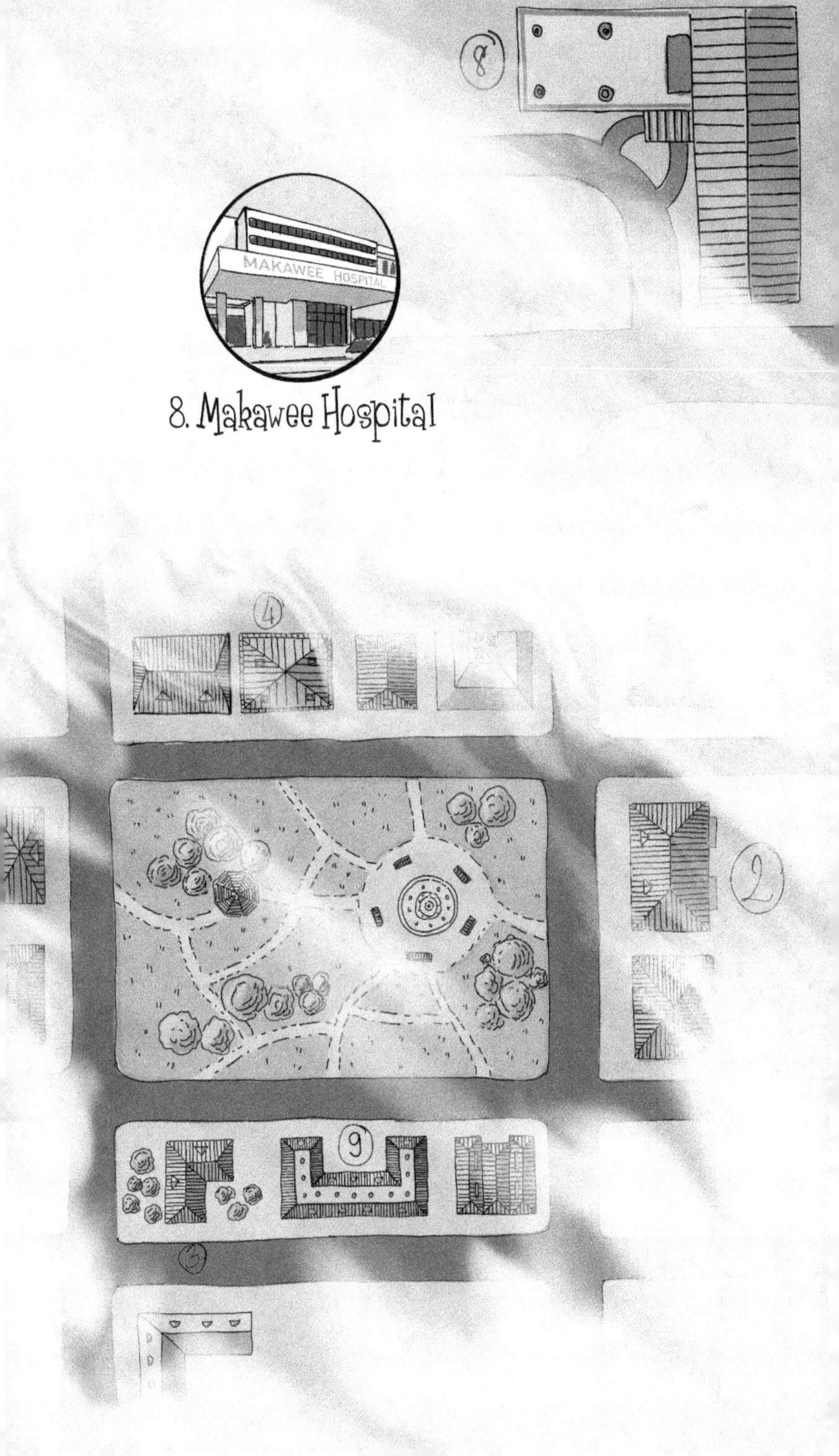

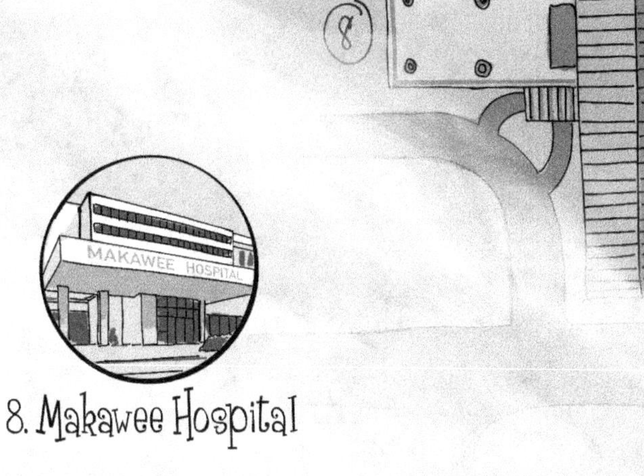

ATLAS
ALMAN

CHAPTER 1

BIG TIME IN FOURTH GRADE

March is a very busy time for fourth grade students in Makawee Elementary School. Every spring, fourth graders are introduced to their first formal research project.

My name is Ginni, and I am in fourth grade. I live with my father—who is a dentist—and my first-grade brother, Frankie, in a small house that is within easy walking distance to school. Makawee is a town of about 15,000 people, and you can walk most anywhere.

It was the first Monday in March, and although all of us knew it was coming, I hoped that maybe the teachers forgot about Research Horror—as some of us call it. Not so. Right after the bell rang that morning, we all settled into our seats.

Ms. Zinger, our homeroom teacher, began, "Boys and girls, today is a big day in the life of a student. Today, you are going to be introduced to your very first formal research assignment. I have two special guests who will be with me momentarily. Together, we will all go through the steps you'll take to complete your research project, and we will also discuss the support we will provide you along your journey."

There were groans all around. Since third grade, we had heard upper classmates bemoan this dreaded research project. Kids told us about the hours and hours it took, looking up all the information and then having to take that data and put it all together in your own words.

"No copying out of Wikipedia, or they'll know," we'd been warned.

Right after the groans died down, we heard a knock on the door. Ms. Zinger opened it, and in walked our guests: Ms. Gynther, our school librarian, and Mrs. Curtz, the librarian for the public library.

"Class, you all know these amazing ladies, Ms. Gynther and Mrs. Curtz," Ms. Zinger said. "They are going to help you with your research. As older students may have told you, you will be researching a famous person. The research will not only be about the person, but we want to know about what the country was like where and when they lived. What was the weather like? What inventions were discovered at the time they lived? To find out information like that, Mrs. Curtz is here to show you how to do it."

Mrs. Curtz held up two big books. Since I sat close to the front of the room, I could read that one said "Atlas" and the other "Almanac."

"In these two books," Mrs. Curtz explained, "and in other similar reference material, I will show you how to find the information that Ms. Zinger is requesting. Over the years, both Ms. Gynther and I have been adding many, many biographies to our library collections, so I'm sure we will be able to provide you with what you need."

She sounded so excited that it almost made me feel like the research project could be kinda fun.

Ms. Gynther stepped in, saying, "And in addition to your book research, I get the fun part of helping you students in the computer lab doing online research. Believe it or not, there are more places to find information other than Wikipedia. I'll show them to you."

Ms. Zinger finished the presentation and gave each of us a packet of information. Along with what she had mentioned before, there was a list of other questions like the birth and death dates (if the person had died), place where they were born, where they lived most of their lives, what they were famous for, etc.

"When you have answered all the questions listed in your packet," she instructed, "you will use the following pages to fill in the outline template I've given you that will help you categorize the information you've found. Then, you can start handwriting your report. After that, Ms. Gynther will take you back to the computer lab and help you print out a picture of your person. Additionally, if any student so wishes, Ms. Gynther is going to keep the lab open after school once we get started so you can type out your report if you choose."

"How long does this stupid report have to be?" Stanley blurted out. Stanley can best be described as our class bully. He calls kids names, picks on everyone, and outside of a few of his cronies, he doesn't have many friends.

"Excuse me? Do you want to raise your hand and re-ask that question, Stanley, with an apology?" Ms. Zinger asked.

Stanley raised his hand. Ms. Zinger called on him, and he said, "I'm sorry, Ms. Zinger. I got overwhelmed. Please tell us how long the report has to be."

We all snickered when Stanley said he got "overwhelmed," but that drew a scowl from Ms. Zinger as well. The snickering soon stopped.

"To answer your question, Stanley, and I'm sure most of you are also wondering, many students have turned in an excellent one-page report. Others have taken two pages to share all their information," Ms. Zinger explained. "Depending upon the person you choose, you may have more or less information to share. What is most important is that the report is in your own words, you've found all the requested information, sentences are clearly written, and that it is interesting for the reader."

"The first page of the packet is a list of noteworthy people to help you get started thinking about who you might want to research," she continued. "By the end of the school day tomorrow, you will meet with me and tell me who you've chosen. That way, you have time to go home tonight and discuss with your family who you might want to research. I'll make sure that no one picks the same famous person. First come, first served."

With that, she said goodbye to the two librarians and asked that we thank them for their time. We all said thank you and gave a short applause.

I knew most of my classmates were dreading the work we were about to have to do, but secretly, I was a tad excited. I had known about Research Horror for a long time since Catherine Pebbles, my best friend, was one grade older than I. In fact, throughout the entire school year, I had in the back of my mind who I might research.

Do I have the guts to research Amelia Earhart? I wondered.

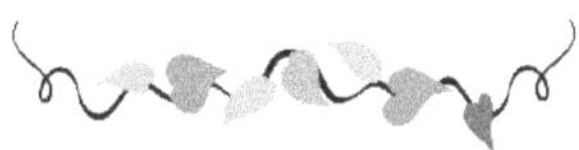

That night as Frankie and I enjoyed a chili dinner, complete with cornbread, I told Dad about Research Horror. I didn't use those exact words, but I know he knew about the project because Catherine and I had talked about it in front of him.

"Well, Dad," I said, "it's time for me to pick my famous person for the research project. I need to let Ms. Zinger know sometime tomorrow."

"Have you given it any thought?" asked Dad.

I looked down at my plate as I answered him. I didn't know what he'd say about my choosing Amelia Earhart, but I knew I needed to tell him before I began. I needed either his support or his advice, if he thought I should choose another person.

Without looking at Dad, I asked, "What do you think about Amelia Earhart?"

"Who's that?" asked Frankie with a mouthful of cornbread.

I had almost forgotten that Frankie was there. Often Frankie doesn't say much, but he is always taking everything in.

Right at that moment, Neelia, our pet kitten, jumped down from her kitchen chair—she had commandeered the chair that Mom had always sat on—and jumped onto my lap. Once on my lap, she leaned up, placed her two paws on my shoulders, and looked directly into my eyes. She gave me a small meow and then leaned her head into my neck.

Dad said, "I think Neelia gave you your answer, Ginni. I think Amelia Earhart would be a good choice for your research project." When I looked up at Dad, I saw a look of love and approval in his eyes.

It was just over two months ago when Neelia entered our family. It was Christmas Eve, and we were simply going through the motions of the holiday season. The summer prior to that Christmas, Mom's plane had been shot down, and she died. Mom had been a fighter pilot for the Air Force, and the hole she left in all our hearts was immense. Christmas had been her favorite holiday, and while we were still trying to have a typical Christmas, it was as if we were sleepwalking through it.

When we were down to the last present, strange things began to happen. The lights mysteriously flickered, Alexa turned on by herself and played "White Christmas" (Mom's favorite holiday song), and a barn owl we now called Tyto knocked on our front door with his beak to call us outside. And there she sat, Neelia, a bundle of black fur, just waiting to be brought into her new home.

Neelia had not only helped us heal the grief we felt by Mom's death, but there was also an undeniable connection she had to Mom. Her fur was the same color as Mom's jet-black hair, her collar she wore when she arrived on our doorstep was purple (Mom's favorite color), and she had taken over the house, like sitting in Mom's chair in the kitchen, as if she belonged there.

So, when she put her paws on my shoulders, it felt as if Mom was telling me, "Yes, do your report on Amelia Earhart."

"You may not know this, Ginni," Dad continued, "but Amelia Earhart was always one of your mom's role models. I know she'd be happy you chose her. But there will be a great deal of research on female pilots and of her mysterious disappearance and whether or not she died on her last flight. Are you sure you can handle all that?"

With every ounce of courage I had, I inhaled a deep breath, then answered, "Yes, I think so." I exhaled. "I've been thinking about this for months, but when I try to come up with another person, my mind always goes back to Amelia Earhart. It seems as if I'm supposed to research her. If you will help when I need it, and if Neelia will help, then I'd like to tell Ms. Zinger tomorrow that I've decided upon her."

"Of course, we'll all help," Dad agreed as he got up from his chair and came over and lovingly kissed the top of my red hair.

Frankie got up and came over, too, and said, "I'll help you too, Ginni. With Neelia, Dad, and me, you'll get an A on this report for sure!"

I laughed as I outstretched my arms and gave a loving hug to my family, with Neelia in the middle.

CHAPTER 2

AMELIA EARHART
IT IS

I had always liked Ms. Zinger. In fact, this fall when I was going back to school after Mom had died, I was full of dread as to what my classmates would say and do. But when the class lists were posted early in August and I saw that I had been assigned to Ms. Zinger, I felt much better. Ms. Zinger has high standards, and she enforces that everyone in her class behaves. I knew that if things got tough and kids teased me about my mom dying, she'd be right by my side.

Thankfully, she never had to intervene. Yes, Stanley had said some pretty mean things throughout the year, but that was to be expected. None of the other kids got involved, though. In fact, they were almost too nice. Too often they'd ask, "How are you doing?" when all I wanted was to simply get through the day. Their questions kept bringing me back to my grief. Like I wanted to continually talk about it—Geesh! I wanted to tell them to leave me alone. Instead, I said I was just fine, and I walked away. I guess they got the hint eventually because they stopped asking.

It was right after recess break, and we were working on a reading assignment, when Ms. Zinger finally had a moment alone at her desk. Boys and girls had been standing there all morning to sign up for their famous person. I looked heavenward, nodded my head, and got out of my seat to walk to her desk. But . . . who came up from behind and pushed me aside? Yep, Stanley.

"Get out of my way, Redhead," he quietly jeered. "I'm going to get to her first!"

What did I care? I thought. *I doubt he is going to choose Amelia Earhart.*

Ms. Zinger had a look of disbelief on her face as Stanley talked with her, but it didn't take too long before I saw her jot a name down on her master list and send him to his seat.

Here I go, I said to myself with every ounce of courage I had.

I stood by her desk as she looked up at me and asked who I wanted to research.

"Amelia Earhart," I said with more confidence than I felt.

Ms. Zinger was obviously startled as she looked at me with more kindness in her eyes than I had ever seen before. She leaned toward me and quietly asked, "Are you sure?"

Gee…I had just gotten over the hump when I talked to Dad about who I wanted to research, but now I had to explain myself again to Ms. Zinger.

"I don't mean to question you, Ginni," Ms. Zinger went on to say, "but I want you to be sure."

"I'm sure," I confirmed. To myself I thought, *Neelia "told" me that it was the thing to do.*

"Well, Ginni, you are stronger than most students I've had the pleasure to teach over my many years in the classroom. If any student can face their past and use it to help them mold a positive future, it is you, my dear." And with that, Ms. Zinger wrote Amelia Earhart next to my name on her master list, nodded her head in approval, and smiled.

"Thank you," I said, as I turned to walk away. I didn't know exactly how to take all of what Ms. Zinger said, but it felt like a compliment.

At noon recess, I told Catherine about what Ms. Zinger had said to me. She, too, asked who I had picked. When I told her Amelia Earhart, she asked, "Are you sure?"

"What is this?!" I said a bit too tersely. "Why is everyone so against my wanting to research a famous person that my mom would have obviously been interested in as well?"

Catherine was a bit taken back by my sharp response, but she just reached for me and gave me a hug. "We all care so much about you, my dear friend. I just hope you are doing this because it's what *you* want to do and not that you think this is who your mom would have wanted you to research."

I sighed and apologized to Catherine. "I'm really sorry, Catherine. But it felt like both Dad and Ms. Zinger gave me the third degree about my choice. The only one who has seemed happy about my pick is Neelia."

Catherine laughed at that. Since she is so close to the family, she knew all about the special connections

Neelia had to each of us. I didn't need to explain my comment.

"Well, my friend, if I can be of any help—looking up information or a shoulder to cry on if things get too heavy—I'm here for you," she offered kindly.

I felt like I needed her shoulder right then and there. But I managed to pull myself together and thank her, telling her that I would most definitely lean on her if needed.

CHAPTER 3

LIBRARY VISIT

Catherine has two younger sisters, Sharnelle and Rose, and the five of us usually walk home together since our houses are right next to each other. You wouldn't get the houses mixed up, however. Since the Pebbles had moved to Makawee from Jamaica several years ago, Ms. Pebbles had decorated their home vibrantly, and their house looked like it should sit on a sandy beach. Why Ms. Pebbles thought that living in Makawee with our long, cold winters instead of a tropical paradise was the better choice for her family, I'll never know. But I'm glad she did; Catherine is the best friend ever.

"There's no time like the present to get started on Research Horror," I announced on our way home. "Who wants to go with me to the public library this afternoon?"

"Oh, Ginni," Catherine bemoaned, "the first time you ask us to help, or at least keep you company, and we can't. Mom is hosting her Book Club tomorrow night, and she'll skin us alive if we don't all have our rooms spic and span. You'd think she was running a hospital at home like she does at work! Not only do we have to clean our rooms, but we have to make sure all of our stuff from the living room and family room is put away *and* clean the bathrooms."

I secretly thought, *I am glad that Dad didn't belong to a Book Club—sounds like too much work to me!*

I answered, "No problem. I just want to get some of the basic information out of the way and check to see what books Mrs. Curtz has. Maybe you can join me later and help when the going gets tough," I suggested with a laugh.

Frankie and I said goodbye to the Pebbles girls and stopped at home to change clothes and grab Neelia. Mrs. Curtz had never been too fond of Neelia in the library, but after looking over the library ordinances, she couldn't find anything that mentioned "no pets." However, we always made sure that Neelia was on her best behavior when we visited.

I texted Dad that we were going to the library to get a start on my research. I love the new cell phone I got after Christmas last year, but now that Dad and I could communicate so easily, he expected me to let him know what was going on with Frankie and me much more than he used to. To every benefit, I guess there's a downside. But to be truthful, I didn't mind too much. Now, when I'm several years older and I start dating, I may feel differently!

We climbed the massive concrete steps to our historic library, and I found out that I wasn't the only one who had decided to get a jump start. The place was full of fourth graders milling around, wide-eyed. I swear that some of them had never been in the library before.

As soon as we walked in, Frankie spotted Scott, the new kid who had moved in with his Grandpa Steve and lived nearby. Frankie and Neelia went over to chat with him. I was glad that his friend was there, because now I didn't have to worry about him getting bored waiting for me—not that he gets bored easily, especially when he has Neelia with him. Wherever Neelia and he go, people love to stop and pet the friendly black kitten. All the while, Frankie just grins. Scott and he had become good friends in just the short time Scott had been in Makawee, and it was good for Frankie to have a guy to pal around with.

I knew that I could get on a computer, or my phone, and look up the basic information on Amelia Earhart from a Google search, but I was curious about other books Mrs. Curtz might have on the shelf. I knew the general direction to head for informational books, and I looked at the posted signs. *Ahh . . . there it was, biographies.*

I laughed as I turned the corner and saw so many fourth graders crammed into the biography section. Mrs. Curtz was there, as was one of her helpers, when I spotted Heather, a shy girl in my class.

"Hey, Heather," I whispered. "I guess everyone thought that today would be a good day to get started."

Heather had a book she was holding close as she looked at the crowd around the bookshelves.

Since biographies are arranged by the last name of the person the book is about, Amelia Earhart was easy to spot since it was near the beginning. There were two books on the shelf, and I grabbed both.

"Who's your famous person?" I asked Heather, once I got back to her after grabbing my books.

She just held her book out for me to read, and I could see it was about Helen Keller. *Interesting choice*, I thought. I smiled at her and nodded.

Just as I was about to compliment her on choosing an amazing person, there was a loud *bang!* Then smaller bangs followed by howls . . . *Wahooooo!*

Everyone standing next to me jumped, and Heather let out a little yelp.

As soon as I got my wits about me, I asked Mrs. Curtz, "What was that?"

"Oh, that?" she blandly said, with a sigh. "That's just our ghost."

"What?" most of us exclaimed.

By now, Frankie and Scott were standing by my side. They, too, must have heard the strange bangs and howls and came to find me. Neelia was struggling to get free, but Frankie held on tightly.

"Well," Mrs. Curtz began, "it started about three weeks ago. The library staff has been hearing bangs, rattles, thumps, and booms—followed by mournful howls and yelps. I can't tell you how many times we have gone upstairs to the attic to search for the noise. I even had some guys from the city maintenance crew stop over and take a look. No one has seen a thing, yet the noises continue."

It may have been my imagination, but Mrs. Curtz seemed to have a bit of a sparkle in her eye when telling us all of this. I think she was enjoying running a haunted library!

"Are you ready to go?" I asked Heather, who was still standing next to me and had gone a little pale.

"Y-Yes . . ." she stammered.

The four of us left the wide-eyed group that was still standing by the biographies, and we headed to the checkout counter. I let Heather go first, and when she was done, she turned to me and quickly whispered, "Goodbye," as she hurried out the front door.

My observant younger brother even noticed Heather's odd behavior and commented, "She was even quieter than usual."

Scott was the first to see Dad walking into the library as I was checking out my books. Frankie hurried to him and excitedly said, "Guess what, Dad? The library is haunted!"

"You don't say . . ." Dad responded with a grin. "That rumor has been going around the downtown businesses for a couple of weeks now. Any ghostly happenings while you guys were here?"

Frankie excitedly told Dad about the loud bangs and bumps we had just heard along with the strange howling.

Frankie concluded, "It was really spooky, Dad. And even Mrs. Curtz said that the library was haunted. No one has been able to find out what is making the noises, and Neelia wasn't happy either!"

Dad got a sly look on his face when Frankie mentioned Mrs. Curtz. "It could be that Mrs. Curtz enjoys having a few extra people coming to the library, hoping that they might hear a ghost. I believe she thinks that it's been good for business."

"Well, Neelia and I don't believe in ghosts... Do we?" Frankie asked while looking at me.

"Of course not, Frankie," I told him. But I secretly wondered, if everything had been searched thoroughly and nothing had been found, what else could it be?

"You got here early, Dad. Did you close the office?" I asked.

Dad nodded his head and told us that it had been a slow day. He had caught up on all his billing, so he sent everyone home early with hopes of catching us at the library.

"How about for dinner we try the new T&T's Pizzeria that opened last week?" he suggested. "We can walk Neelia home. Scott, I'll call your grandfather, and I bet he'd love to have the two of you join us."

"Great!" shouted Scott. "I love pizza!"

CHAPTER 4

PIZZA AND MYSTERY NUMBER 2

Our owl, Tyto, followed us on our trek toward home which took us past Yummy Tummy Grocery, and who should I see coming out of the store? Mr. Smiley from Smiley's Auto World and Irving from Handyman's Hardware. Last month, Frankie and I had canvassed much of Makawee to get signatures on a petition to save Sweet Georgina's Chocolate Shoppe. And I'm happy to report that we were successful. Knocking on Mr. Smiley's door for his signature was one of the highlights of that adventure. Not only is Mr. Smiley handsome, but he's on TV!

It looked like Mr. Smiley and Irving were in the middle of a heated argument. Both men had scowls on their faces. As soon as we got into earshot, I could hear Irving say, "But, Smiley, a trannie shouldn't go out, even on a used car, at only 63,000 miles. You sold me a lemon, and I want you to do something about it."

As soon as Mr. Smiley noticed that we were near, his scowl left his face, and it was replaced by his TV grin. "Why, Jim," he said, "you have quite a little group with you today." And with that, he bent down, giving Neelia some scritches on her cheek.

Dad replied, "Yep, I found this lot at our haunted library and decided we should try out the new pizzeria."

"As I was saying . . . " interrupted Irving, "what about that lemon of a Chrysler you sold me?"

"What?" asked Mr. Smiley, who appeared to be in a daze while petting Neelia. "Oh, yes, the transmission. Bring it on in Irv, and we'll fix or replace it—on the house. Can't have a transmission go out at only 63,000 miles, now can we? That's just not right."

Irving looked surprised, but he agreed that he'd be there first thing in the morning. I imagined that he wanted to act quickly before Mr. Smiley changed his mind.

We all went our separate ways. I looked back at Mr. Smiley and heard him mutter, "Why did I just say that?" He was staring at Neelia with a most quizzical expression on his attractive face.

Out of the corner of my eye, I spotted a wayward black puppy. I could swear I had seen that puppy hanging around town, but I wasn't able to spot a collar. Dad was marching us straight home, so I would have to investigate this later.

In no time at all, we were back downtown, minus Neelia, but with Grandpa Steve instead. Usually, our little group was comprised of Catherine and her sisters when we would do things. Since Frankie and Scott were busy talking, and Dad and Steve were catching up on Makawee's happenings, I felt like the odd person out. This reinforced my earlier thought that it truly was a good thing for Frankie to have a boy his own age around. He must have often felt like the odd person out when I was busy talking with the girls.

We walked into T&T's Pizzeria and were greeted by Ms. T herself. I had learned from Dad that the Ts had recently moved to Makawee to start a pizzeria. The Ts are called that because of their names: Mr. Terry and Ms. Terri. They had retired from their corporate jobs and liked the idea of keeping busy with a small-town business. Our previous pizza place had recently closed, so the entire town was happy that they came along to provide us with fresh-baked pizza pies.

"Sit anywhere you'd like," said Ms. T as she flitted about.

We grabbed a booth in the back. After a few minutes, we were served one of the most delicious pizzas I've ever tasted.

"They shouldn't have any problem staying in business with pizza that good," Dad commented as we all walked home.

"Yes!" answered Scott, who for once had a carefree look on his face.

We didn't know why Scott was living with his grandfather, but there had to be something serious going on since he wasn't living with his parents. Neither Scott nor Grandpa Steve had shared anything with us yet, and we may never know. But Scott seemed sad and lost much of the time, so it was good to watch him laughing and goofing around with Frankie on our walk home.

Dad and I headed into the house right after Frankie announced that he was going to say hi to Tyto before he came in.

When I peeked out the living room window, there was Tyto, swooping around Frankie as he laughed and jumped at the owl.

I went upstairs to pay some attention to my little pet, Mr. Whiskers. Mr. Whiskers had also joined us during last Christmas. He had been stealing small items connected to Mom over break, and Neelia was the one who finally found all the items tucked away under the Christmas tree skirt, proudly guarded by Mr. Whiskers. There is no normal cat versus mouse problem between Neelia and Mr. Whiskers. All three of our newfound animal friends are best buddies.

I was almost ready to put Mr. Whiskers back into his cage and get into my jammies when Frankie pounded on my door.

"What is it?" I asked, noticing the concerned look on his face.

"Come outside, and I'll show you!" he nervously said.

"Okay, okay, give me a second," I replied.

Frankie raced downstairs after I had put Mr. Whiskers to bed. I grabbed my jacket, and we went outside.

We didn't go far. Frankie led me to the bushes that are right under the living room window. It didn't take but a second for me to see what had Frankie so worked up. There, as clear as day, were many footprints right under the window—as if someone had been standing outside peering in.

"Ginni, your hair!" Frankie exclaimed.

I looked down at the hair falling over my shoulder, and I was doing it again. I had a habit of twirling my hair on my finger every time there was a mystery afoot.

"Is it the footprints?" asked Frankie. "Or the ghost in the library?"

Frankie knew of my strange habit and often caught me twirling my hair when I was unaware of what I was doing.

"I don't know, Frankie," I said. "It could be both."

"Oh, boy! Two mysteries!" uttered Frankie.

"But this is not good, Frankie," I went on to say. "Remember just last month Stanley had been following us around with his drone? I wonder if, even though he got caught, he didn't learn his lesson. Before we tell Dad, tomorrow after school, let's demand that Stanley stop over, and we'll confront him."

When we were back in the house and both Frankie and I had settled into bed, I couldn't help but go over the conversation that Dad, Frankie, and I had with Stanley and his dad just a couple of weeks ago when we caught Stanley with his drone. Stanley had been embarrassed, and he doesn't get embarrassed often, even when he gets caught doing nasty things. I couldn't imagine he'd still be doing something like peering in our living room window—but if not Stanley, who else could it be?

CHAPTER 5

SICK IN BED

When I awoke the following morning, I knew I wasn't going anywhere. My throat was on fire, and I was hot and sweaty. I wrapped my robe around me and padded downstairs to find Dad.

"Dad," I weakly said, "I'm not going to make it to school today."

I was never one to "play sick" and try to get out of school, so it took only one look from Dad to confirm that I was going right back to bed.

"I'll bring up some oatmeal and juice, Ginni," Dad said, "and I'll call the office to have them cancel my appointments for the day."

"Oh, no," I cried, "you don't have to cancel your appointments. Dad, I'm ten years old, I can stay home alone and sleep. I'll keep my cell phone right by the nightstand, and I promise to call you if I need anything."

Dad came up a few minutes later with my breakfast on a tray and the thermometer. After I held it in my mouth for what seemed like forever, he took it from me and announced it was 99.7°.

"Well, that confirms it, Ginni. I'm staying home with you."

"Oh, Dad," I cried, "you really don't have to!"

"Not your decision, sweetheart. You are my little girl, and I'm going to take care of you," Dad lovingly said.

At that moment, Frankie walked in and asked what was going on.

Dad immediately got up from my bedside and walked over to Frankie, telling him to not come in any further. "Your sister isn't feeling well today, and she is going to stay home. You'd better stay away from her in case she's contagious."

Frankie had a very sympathetic look on his face, reminding me once again just how sensitive my younger brother could be.

"I'll be okay, Frankie," I told him in a raspy voice. "I just need to sleep."

Frankie, who had Neelia in his arms, set her down and told her to watch over me. She immediately came to my bed, jumped up, and nuzzled by my head.

As I petted her and rolled over, I couldn't help but think that I had no time to be sick—not with two mysteries on my mind and a research report to do. *I'm sure I'll feel better tomorrow,* I told myself.

But little did I know . . .

I slept straight through to lunch, when Dad stepped into my room to check in on me. "I'm sorry I don't have time to make your grandmother's famous chicken soup with homemade pasta noodles," he told me as I was waking up. "But I'll heat up a can of chicken noodle soup and butter some crackers for you."

I sure wished I was feeling better, but it was just the opposite. I felt hotter, and my throat hurt even more.

When Neelia heard Dad stepping into my room, she left my pillow and went to the foot of the bed where she sat straight and tall as if she wanted to say something to Dad.

Before he left to make lunch, he got the thermometer again and stuck it in my mouth. When he took out the thermometer and looked at it, he stepped out in the hallway. Even though he was outside my room, I still heard him making a call to Ms. Pebbles for medical advice. She is the Director of Nursing at the Makawee Hospital, and it wasn't the first time we've relied upon her.

When he stepped back into my room, he said, "Put on some sweats, honey. I'm taking you to urgent care."

When I started to protest that I'd be just fine if I could sleep a bit more, I got the "Dad Look." The look that says, *Don't argue, and do what I say.*

After dressing, I opened the cage door and patted Mr. Whiskers on his little head, then Neelia and I left my room and slowly made our way downstairs. After saying goodbye to Neelia, Dad helped me get into the car—I couldn't believe how weak I felt—and we drove the few blocks to the hospital with Tyto following behind.

Ms. Pebbles must have informed the receptionist that we were coming in, because we were ushered right past the front desk and into an exam room.

I was told to lie on the table that had white paper stretched on it and some nice person took my temperature (again), put an arm band around my left arm, and placed a little white cap thingy on my pointer finger. *All this for a sore throat,* I thought. The nurse left and said the doctor would be in shortly.

After that, I felt a little rustle in my pocket. I had felt a rustle like that before. Could it be?

Yes! I reached my hand down, and I immediately knew that Mr. Whiskers was right beside me, because I felt his long whiskers brushing against my hand. He was curled up in my pocket against my left hip while Dad was sitting on my right.

How in the world did Mr. Whiskers get in my pocket? I wondered. It must have been when I reached in his cage to pet him goodbye. He must have jumped from the cage and slipped into my sweats pocket. While I wondered what kind of trouble this might cause, it was very comforting having him by my side.

I must have been dozing, because Dad was gently nudging my shoulder, telling me the doctor was here. When I looked around, I saw the doctor flipping through papers on a clipboard. When he noticed I was looking at him, he gently leaned forward to introduce himself.

"Hello, Ginni, I'm Dr. Lebeau. I'm here to figure out why your throat is so sore," he kindly explained.

He then turned to Dad and said that he was going to do a couple of tests to find out if I may have strep throat or tonsillitis. "Has Ginni had many sore throats in the past year or so?" he asked Dad.

"None like this one," answered Dad, "but thinking over the year, I guess I remember Ginni mentioning a sore throat occasionally. Ginni?"

I closed my eyes, and my thoughts went completely to what this past year had been like. Losing Mom last summer, trying to adjust to home and school, and trying to learn how to move on without her was almost more than I could handle. Who had time to worry about a sore throat? But I tried to focus on the question, and I realized that yes, I had suffered a couple of times this past year with a sore throat.

After all this thinking, I reported to the doctor that I had had some sore throats lately, but nothing like I had now.

"Good to know," Dr. Lebeau said. "Well, I'm going to swab the back of your throat and get a culture to help us see what might be causing the infection. Then I'm going to send in a blood guy to draw a small sample to check on your blood cell count. Sound okay?"

I simply nodded my head. It's not like I was going to tell him no.

The doctor reached into a cupboard behind me and drew out a very long Q-tip. "This will be a bit uncomfortable, but it'll last for just a second. Open your mouth wide for me please."

Wow! I had forgotten how I hated having that done. I hadn't had to have a throat swab too terribly often in the past, and I hoped not to have another in a good, long time. Very unpleasant. I'm just glad I didn't gag and throw up on the doctor.

After the swab, the doctor looked down my throat with his light, as well as into my eyes and ears. He listened to my heart, made sure I bounced my knees when he hit them with his little hammer, and felt all around my neck with a gentle touch.

"I'll send in the blood guy shortly," said Dr. Lebeau as he left the room.

"Thanks, Doc," Dad said. I could tell that he was worried as he nodded good-bye to Dr. Lebeau.

It wasn't even ten minutes later when I heard a cart being wheeled down the hall and into my room.

"Hello, Ginni," said a nice-looking young man as he pushed the cart into my room. "I'm here to take a small sample of blood."

Maybe this hospital won't be so bad if all the guys are as cute as this guy and the doctor, I giggled to myself.

"If you don't mind, I'm going to use your other arm," he told me as he passed by the foot of my bed. "It's closer to the window, and I can see your veins better."

As I looked out window, Tyto was sitting in a nearby tree as if on guard duty.

Just then Mr. Whiskers, who was tucked on that side of me, started to scurry. I bet he heard the cart move to that side and was worried about being discovered. As the tech lifted the blanket to reach my arm, Mr. Whiskers ran over my legs and off the bed. I let out a gasp as I saw him race out the door.

"It'll be okay, honey," Dad said as he came to my side to pat my other arm. "It won't hurt much."

Obviously, I couldn't tell Dad what was bothering me. I didn't care about being poked; I was just terribly worried about Mr. Whiskers. But I knew I couldn't do anything at this point, and I didn't want to have to explain myself, so I just closed my eyes and told myself to relax.

I started thinking about how long Mr. Whiskers had been in our house stealing little items and stuffing them under the Christmas tree skirt and he hadn't gotten hurt then. Plus, he went with me, tucked in my scarf, when we were getting signatures to save Sweet Georgina's Chocolate Shoppe and hadn't gotten in trouble. After that, I even made him a mouse-size scarf of his very own. *He'll be fine,* I said silently to comfort myself.

But just then, I heard a loud scream and right after that a crash that sounded as if a complete set of pots and pans had fallen on the floor.

Then someone shouted, "*Eeekk!* A mouse!"

And then there were more screeches and shuffling sounds.

Oh no, I thought, *Mr. Whiskers didn't get away unseen. He'll be fine, he'll be fine, he'll be fine . . .*

Last Christmas, when we were worried that Neelia might have to go back to her original owner, Dad had shared with me the power of believing. I must admit that I've relied on "believing" more than once since then, and this was going to be another time. *Mr. Whiskers will be just fine; I believe Mr. Whiskers will return to me.*

Then from somewhere further down the hall, I heard another loud clang and bang with more shrieks, and a small tear fell from my eye as I worried about my dear friend.

It was then that Ms. Pebbles stepped into my room with a huge grin on her face. "Hi, you two," she said, "I came to check in to see how things were going, but I never thought I'd see a show on the way down. You won't believe it, but somehow a mouse has gotten in the hallway and is running for his dear life! You should see the ruckus he's causing. Supply trolleys are being rolled out of the way, a huge cart of bedpans was tipped over, and you'd think that some people had never seen a mouse before. I know I should be chagrined about a mouse being in the hospital, but it's the cutest little thing you ever did see. In fact, he's carrying what looks like a scrap of yarn, and it looks as if he has a scarf around his neck."

At that, Dad gave me a great big scowl. "Well, I'm sure he'll head outside at the quickest opportunity," Dad said to Ms. Pebbles. But he continued to give me the "Dad Look."

Ms. Pebbles felt my forehead, and she, too, asked me about the number of sore throats I had over the past year. Even without knowing where Mr. Whiskers might have gone, I found myself drifting off to sleep again after she left.

I don't know how long I was asleep this time before Dad was again rocking my shoulder to wake me. Dr. Lebeau was standing right next to Dad.

"Ginni," Dr. Lebeau said, "you have tonsillitis. With your history of sore throats this past year and the severity of this infection, your dad and I have decided that it'd be best for us to remove your tonsils. After about two weeks, you'll be back to normal as if nothing had happened, and you shouldn't have these recurring sore throats anymore. Does this sound okay to you?"

I couldn't quite get this all through my head. "You mean I'm going to have an operation?" I asked in a scared voice.

Dad immediately grabbed my hand and gave me an assuring grip. "Yes, honey, but they do this surgery all the time. It'll be a piece of cake for my brave girl," he assured me.

I looked at the doctor and nodded my head. I didn't trust that I could speak without a tear slipping down my cheek.

"Good," said Dr. Lebeau, "but now the bad news. The operating rooms are a bit busy today, so I can't get Ginni's surgery scheduled until late this afternoon. Normally, it's a same-day surgery, but with her heightened infection, and the late surgery, I'd like her to stay overnight in the hospital. Is that okay with you guys?"

Dad told the doctor that this would be fine, but all I could think of was that it meant more of a delay until I could search for Mr. Whiskers.

Right after the doctor left, Dad told me that he needed to sign some papers to get everything lined up for the surgery, and then he had to pick Frankie up from school. "While you were dozing, Ms. Pebbles and I made arrangements that Frankie would stay with the girls while I was here with you. But I want to go tell him what's all going on and assure him that you'll be just fine. You know he'll be worried." He leaned over, kissed my cheek, and told me to simply get some more rest. "I'll be back before you know it," he said as we waved goodbye.

As soon as he left, a tear trickled down the cheek that Dad had just kissed. As I reached up to wipe it away, the dam burst, and I seriously started crying. I was nervous about surgery, worried about Frankie worrying about me, and seriously concerned about the safety of Mr. Whiskers. Also, while I have the best dad ever, there are still times when I miss Mom terribly. All I wanted right then was for Mom to be by my side telling me everything would be okay. I reached for part of the pillow to cover my face so that no one would hear my sobbing when suddenly, I felt a small tug and pull of the covers. I peeked under the covers, and there was Mr. Whiskers, once again sitting by my hip. It looked like he was grinning ear to ear.

"Oh my!" I cried. "Where have you been, my dear little friend?" While he still had on his little scarf, it looked a bit disheveled. I straightened it for him, picked him up, and gave him a great big nuzzle.

What was I going to do with him while I was in surgery? I thought. "Should Dad take you home?" I asked Mr. Whiskers. I must have been sicker than I thought, for it looked to me like he was going to cry. "How about you hide until I get out of surgery?"

With that comment, Mr. Whiskers simply laid down on my pillow next to my head. "Ok, then," I said, "just don't get into trouble."

I am having a conversation with my pet mouse, I thought, *and he's answering me.* However, I was too tired to worry about my sanity. Now that Mr. Whiskers was lying next to me, I no longer needed to cry. I realized that Dad would take good care of Frankie and that the doctors would take good care of me. And somehow, I knew Mom was by my side as well. What comfort it is to have those you love near you.

By the time Dad got back from picking up Frankie, we didn't have long to wait until it was surgery time. Two nurses came into the room wheeling a metal table. In a jiffy, they had picked me up using the blanket I was lying on, gently placed me on the metal table, and I was ready to be wheeled away to the operating room. I looked back at my bed, and there was Mr. Whiskers, with only his nose and eyes peeking out from under the blanket. I glanced out the window, and Tyto was still sitting in the nearby tree.

"Oh!" Dad exclaimed. "I almost forgot!" He placed Frankie's origami black cat in my hand—the same cat that Frankie had made last Christmas when we first found Neelia. "Frankie wanted you to have Neelia watching over you, too."

That was all it took. The tears started flowing again. It was scary to be on this cold, metal table, getting ready to be wheeled away for surgery.

"Don't cry, honey," Dad said with a couple of tears in his own eyes. "It'll all be over before you know it. And then . . . you can have as much ice cream as you want!" I smiled at that.

As I held on to the paper Neelia and glanced one last time at Mr. Whiskers and Tyto, I knew all would be fine. Dad walked me down as far as they let him, and the woman who was pushing my cart gently told me that Dad would have to hang onto my paper cat because it couldn't come into the operating room.

Dad took the origami Neelia and kissed my forehead, and they wheeled me off.

The only thing I remember about the surgery was trying to count backward from 100 after they gave me the sleeping medication. I think I made it to 97 before I was out. In what seemed like minutes later, the surgery was done, and I drowsily woke up back in my hospital room. I got a hug and kiss from Dad, secretly petted Mr. Whiskers who obviously did manage to hide while I was in surgery, nodded to Tyto, and glanced at the paper Neelia sitting on the table by my bed before I shut my eyes again.

Never thought I'd be having a day like this when I woke up.

CHAPTER 6

SLOWLY BACK TO NORMAL

Dad was sitting in the chair next to my bed when I awoke the next morning. "How are you feeling?" he asked the minute he saw me open my eyes.

I opened my mouth as if to answer him but thought better of it. My throat wasn't on fire like it had been yesterday, but it was very sore and uncomfortable. I managed to squeak out, "Okay," and nodded my head.

Just then Dr. Lebeau stepped in, and he, too, asked how I was doing. I had learned my lesson, so I just gave him the thumbs up sign. He smiled and said, "I see you have learned to lessen the amount of talking. Hand signals will be great for communicating these next couple of days, as well as texting. But after a day or two, it shouldn't hurt to talk. But no straining your voice for the next couple of weeks. And no hard physical exertion. We don't want to strain any muscles and start your throat bleeding."

After that advice, he gave me a quick look over all the while telling Dad that the surgery went very well. "I'm glad we made the decision to remove the tonsils. They were extremely inflamed and would only continue to give Ginni problems," he said as he left the room.

"The nurse who was in earlier while you were sleeping, Ginni, said they were ready for you to check out as soon as you had a bite and were wide awake," Dad said. "Feel like some apple juice and oatmeal?"

"I'll try," I squeaked out. I was now awake enough to think about Mr. Whiskers. I reached down by my hip, and there he was. As soon as he felt my hand, he rubbed his little nose on it. I smiled as I tickled him back.

Dad was told that the earliest I could go back to school was next week on Wednesday. That seemed like a lifetime! Didn't he know I had a report to write, a ghost mystery to solve, and to track down the person who had made those footprints outside the front window? All this couldn't wait a week.

When my eyes got big and I opened my mouth, Dad told me to hush. "I knew you'd be unhappy about missing this much school, Ginni. You're not like most kids who'd love to have a week off from school. But I already talked to Ms. Zinger, and she's putting together a packet of work for you to do so you can stay on top of things. And the doctor said you can do as much schoolwork as you feel up to. I want no arguments about this, but tomorrow Bonnie is going to stay with you. I best start tending to some teeth!"

I opened my mouth, saw the "Dad Look" (again), and simply shut my mouth. I knew it wasn't going to do any good to argue, and I didn't have the voice for it anyway. I just shut my eyes and rested my head back on the pillow. Besides, Bonnie, who helped us when we were petitioning for Sweet Georgina's, is pretty cool.

It was about noon when I got back to the house, and Mr. Whiskers managed to stay hidden in my pocket all during the wheelchair ride down the hall and the transfer to the car. Ms. Pebbles had stopped to check in right before Dad wheeled me out of the room and told Dad to call on her day or night if I took a turn for the worse or if he needed anything. I agreed with Dad who thanked her and told her that, hopefully, the worse was now over.

Tyto, of course, accompanied us home. As soon as I walked into the house, there was Neelia pawing at my leg wanting to be picked up. "Wait," said Dad as he reached down to pick her up and place her in my arms. Remember, no physical exertion." Although I didn't think that picking up a 6-pound kitten was too much exertion, I guess I was going to have to put up with being babied for a couple of days.

Immediately, Mr. Whiskers used his tiny claws to crawl out from my pocket, up my sweats, to meet up with Neelia. She licked his little face and it felt like they were talking to each other, with Neelia mewing and Mr. Whiskers squeaking. *I must still be feeling the effect of the sleeping medication*, I thought. *Now I'm thinking I'm hearing a cat and a mouse talk to one another!*

It was about an hour and half after school got out that the Pebbles girls all stopped over. Frankie was sitting next to me on the couch, where Dad had made a recovery bed with a bunch of pillows, blankets, and a TV tray nearby that held the remote, ice water, and a puzzle book of find-a-words. Frankie wasn't saying much, but we were both comforted by petting Neelia, who was snuggled in my lap. Dad had made me put Mr. Whiskers back in his cage for a much-needed rest.

Immediately, I knew that something was going on with the Pebbles' visit. As soon as they slipped off their coats, I saw that both Catherine and Sharnelle had put on their mother's scrubs. While those two, with a bunch of safety pins to tighten things up, could get the scrubs to stay on, poor Rose would have drowned in them. So instead, Rose had on a pair of footed jammies. Catherine came in carrying a little black bag and took charge.

"Miss," she asked, "where is the Mus musculus?"

"Huh?" I answered. And then it dawned on me. Dad had used the scientific name of a house mouse back when we first found Mr. Whiskers. I giggled and pointed upstairs to my bedroom.

"Ms. Sharnelle, you may begin your checkup while I retrieve the traumatized patient," Catherine said with authority. "And, Ms. Rose, please be ready to perform your duties as well."

Catherine had always wanted to be a veterinarian, and Sharnelle had always thought she'd like to be a nurse someday, so both over the years had gotten medical toys. The three of them each carried their own little "medical kit" bags.

While Catherine ran upstairs, Sharnelle took out of her black bag a real stethoscope—it helps to have a mom who's a nurse—and started listening to my heart. Meanwhile, Rose took out a huge bundle of Ace bandages and started to wrap it around and around my head and throat.

As she was starting this, I heard Sharnelle whisper in her ear, "Remember, not too tight, she just had surgery."

Ahh, I thought, *this was all planned. How sweet of my dear friends!*

As Catherine was coming down the stairs with Mr. Whiskers sitting on her shoulder, Sharnelle was just finishing her examination and Rose had my entire head and neck (except for my nose and eyes) all bandaged up.

I must have been a sight, for Catherine burst out laughing when she saw me. Catherine isn't one to heartedly laugh without a good reason. She immediately whipped out her cell phone and started taking picture after picture.

"Here," Frankie said, "you get in the picture, Catherine, with Mr. Whiskers, and I'll take a picture of all of you.

Just as he was snapping away, Dad walked in from his home office.

He, too, burst out laughing. "I was busy in my office and didn't even hear you girls come in," Dad said when he was able to talk. "So nice to have the EMT Pebbles crew stop by!"

That event was the highlight of the following three days. All weekend long, I did nothing but watch some movies, do some word puzzles, and doze with Neelia and Mr. Whiskers lying on me. Dad did set a card table up in the living room. Frankie and I started on a big puzzle, but I didn't have the concentration to sit there for any length of time.

By Monday, I felt more like myself, and it was sad to see Frankie head off to school shortly after Dad had left for the office. Bonnie did her best to cheer me up, but all I could think about was everything I would be missing. Before Frankie left for school, I did make a plan with him. I told him to somehow talk with Stanley and give him this note from me.

"What is it?" Frankie had asked.

"Well, here's what I'm thinking, Frankie. Since I can't leave the house to go to school or the library to work on my report or to investigate the supposed library ghost, the only other mystery to work on is the one at home," I explained.

"Who left the footprints, you mean?" asked Frankie.

"Yes," I answered. "My note tells Stanley to come to the house right after school and that I want to talk with him."

"You think that'll work? Will he really come over?" Frankie asked doubtingly.

"You know how big Stanley's ego is, Frankie. Believe me, he'll stop over. He'll be too curious not to," I said. "And somehow, I'll have to get Bonnie out of the house while he's here. No reason to drag her into all of this."

"Okay," Frankie said. "I'm sure I can catch him during recess, if not even before school."

Now that the plan was in motion, I simply had to figure out exactly what I'd say to Stanley when he got here.

The day didn't drag on like I expected. I felt well enough to work a bit on my Amelia Earhart report. I was able to find and write down all the easy stuff, like when she was born, what she was famous for, what inventions were created during her lifetime, and some other things. I even found a hidden fact that I had never heard of before, and I hoped that neither had Ms. Zinger.

Neelia never left my side during the entire day, and Bonnie had kept herself busy cooking in the kitchen. Early in the afternoon, the three of us took a break and watched a movie together. And I had come up with a decent plan, I hoped, to get Bonnie out of the house at the time when Frankie would be bringing Stanley home.

It was now 3:05. Time to put the plan in motion.

"Bonnie!" I called from the couch as loud as my hoarse voice would allow. Immediately, Bonnie came rushing in. "Ginni, dear!" she gasped. "Don't use your voice that way! Tomorrow, I'm going to bring over a bell, so you don't have to call out. But what can I do for you now, sweetie?"

"I'm sorry, Bonnie. You're right," I admitted. "I should have gotten up and gone to the kitchen. Anyway, would you go to Chilly Willy's Ice Cream Shop and get me one of their special Tornado Twirlers? I've been craving a raspberry Twirler all afternoon."

"Hmmm . . ." Bonnie said. "Are you sure you'll be okay while I'm gone?"

"It'll only take you a few minutes. I'll be fine," I said.

"Oh, you're right," Bonnie answered. "I guess I'm just being a little overprotective. I'll hurry and be right back."

"Take your time . . ." I said after her as she left the room to get her purse. "I'm not going anywhere."

As I said this, I could see Frankie and Stanley marching up the sidewalk. I quickly ran and got Neelia's harness and leash, so we'd be ready. Frankie was taking long strides in order to keep up with Stanley. Bonnie was out the back door and on her way, just at the time Frankie was on the front steps with Stanley.

I stepped out with Neelia in tow. She immediately went straight to Frankie, who picked her up and they nuzzled. And as if on cue, Tyto began circling overhead as well. We had quite the gang ready to confront Stanley.

"What's this all about, Carrot Top?" Stanley crossly asked. "Did you miss me so much from your sick bed that you had to call me over?"

I didn't bother to respond, just rolled my eyes and said, "Would you please step over here?" And with that, I led him behind the bushes to the footsteps that were still in the dirt. Luckily, it hadn't rained, so all of us could see the footprints clearly.

"Ya, so?" Stanley said. I could tell he was a bit confused by what was going on.

I urged, "Come on, Stanley! 'Fess up. We don't have much time before Bonnie gets back. I know you made those footprints while peeking in our picture window. Just like you were tracking me with your drone. Didn't you learn your lesson?"

"W-w-what?" Stanley stammered. "Why would I be looking in your window?"

"For the same reason you were following me with your drone. Although I don't really know the reason why you did that, either," I had to admit.

"Now, look here. These are not my footprints, I swear!" Stanley said.

I had to admit, Stanley was either doing a great job of acting, or he was really telling the truth and they weren't his footprints.

Stanley went over to one set of the footprints and placed his foot right next to the track in the dirt. As soon as he did this, Neelia wiggled out of Frankie's arms and went over to Stanley, rubbing her body against his legs. Begrudgingly, Stanley reached down and picked her up. At this time, Tyto flew back into the trees.

"See?" he said. "The footprints are at least three sizes smaller than my foot. I couldn't have possibly made those. Even your stupid cat doesn't think I made the prints, since she's been nuzzling me ever since I picked her up."

And to prove his point, he pressed down in the hard dirt to make an impression of his tennis shoe.

Stanley was absent-mindedly petting Neelia all the while he was showing us his clodhopper-sized footprint.

"*Humph*," was all I could say. And just then, I heard a car coming down the street. "That's Bonnie with my raspberry Twirler. Quick, Stanley! You'd better head home."

Stanley had just rounded the corner of the house, and Frankie and I sat down on the front steps as if we'd been sitting there all along.

"Hi, Frankie!" Bonnie called out. "I got a Twirler for you, too. I hope you like peppermint!"

Frankie grinned, because peppermint was his favorite, and the three of us walked back inside to enjoy our ice cream treats.

Bonnie stayed until Dad got home, and by then, it was time for dinner. Frankie and I didn't have time to talk about the footprints until bedtime.

I'd been going to bed early since the surgery. Once Dad had tucked us both in and had gone downstairs, Frankie sneaked out of his room, and he and Neelia climbed up onto my bed.

"I don't know what to think, Frankie," I said as I slipped out from under the covers and brought Mr. Whiskers to the bed to play with Neelia. "Obviously, Stanley isn't the one sneaking around the house making the footprints. He's right—the prints are at least three sizes smaller than his shoe print. But who else could it be?"

"Now that we know how big of a footprint Stanley makes, it has to be someone more my size," Frankie suggested.

"Frankie, that's brilliant!" I exclaimed. "Yes, I've had my mind on someone in my class or even Catherine's, but you're absolutely right! It does have to be someone much younger who would wear a smaller shoe size."

Frankie beamed at my compliment. *I'll have to acknowledge Frankie more often,* I thought. *Mom was always so good at building up both of our self-esteems. Now it's up to me to remember to do this for Frankie.*

"I can't imagine someone in your class peeping through our windows, though. Do you have a girlfriend who's spying on you?" I teased.

Frankie just gave me a scowl, but I did notice he blushed a bit.

"Well, this puts a whole new spin on things. I'll need to sleep on it. I can't believe how tired I get since the surgery. You and Neelia had best go to bed, and I'll try and see what I can come up with," I told Frankie.

"Do you want me to put Mr. Whiskers in his cage for you?" asked Frankie.

I shook my head and said, "Since Mr. Whiskers was so good in the hospital and stayed close to my side, I'm not worried about his running away. I think he can have more freedom. Plus, I think he likes sleeping next to me." And to prove my point, Mr. Whiskers laid down close to my neck. Before Frankie even got out of my room, I was fast asleep.

ATTIC

CHAPTER 7

AMELIA EARHART . . . DONE

Tuesday morning, I woke up feeling like my old self. "Can I *pleasssse* go to school today?" I begged Dad.

"No," Dad sternly said. "You'll follow doctor's orders and stay home until tomorrow."

"How about a compromise?" I asked.

While I didn't get the "Dad Look" in response, it was close.

"How about Bonnie and I take a nice leisurely visit to the library today so I can finish up my report?" I asked. "I need to find information in the almanac and atlas, and then I'll have everything ready to start writing the report from my notes. Really, Dad, how stressful can a library visit be?"

"Have you forgotten about the ghost? Could be a dangerous place," Dad said with a wink.

I had him! As soon as I can get Dad to joke about something, then I can almost always talk him into what I want.

Just then, Bonnie knocked on the back door, opened it, and hollered, "Yoo-hoo!"

"Come in, Bonnie!" Dad called back.

When she had settled inside, and after I had continued to show Dad my pleading eyes, Dad sighed and asked, "Bonnie, do you think you can keep our restless little girl calm enough to go to the library so that she can look up the information she needs to finish her report on Amelia Earhart? I swear, I've never seen a kid so driven before."

"Amelia Earhart?" Bonnie asked with alarm in her voice. "Honey, how are you holding up, doing a report on Amelia Earhart?"

I sighed. I should be used to everyone second guessing my famous person choice by now, but it still hurt every time someone asked. It was like when the school year started this year, and everyone kept asking me if I was doing okay. But as I got to thinking about it, this could be one of the reasons why Dad was worried about me taking on this famous person—not just the research, but everyone's reactions. *Hmmmm . . . smart man, my dad. I'll just have to continue to buck up and let everyone know that it's okay.*

Dad looked at me. I told Bonnie that Neelia told me that it would be a good choice for my book report, and then I left to gather my notes and things for the library. When I left the room, I saw Bonnie glance at Dad with a most quizzical expression, and I just grinned. My heart warmed when I overheard Bonnie tell Dad, "Aileen would be so proud of her."

"Yes," Dad replied. "You're right. Her mom would be very proud."

In no time at all, we were pulling up to the library. Somehow, I had managed to convince Bonnie to let me bring Neelia along. As we were getting ready to go, she was meowing wildly, and I knew she really wanted to join us.

"You know, Bonnie," I said, "we could have walked."

"I have my orders, too, my dear," said Bonnie.

"Your dad said, 'No exertion,' and I'm taking him at his word."

I just shook my head as Bonnie drove into the handicapped spot and told me to get out while she parked the car in a non-handicapped space. *Adults!*

I started walking up the library steps, when out of the corner of my eye, I saw that stray, black puppy again. I gingerly started walking back down the steps to ease my way over to the stray, but it bolted away. I sighed as he ran from me, and I heard Neelia quietly mew as well.

I walked back up the steps and found Mrs. Curtz working at the front desk. She frowned at Neelia, but didn't say anything other than, "Ginni, didn't you just have your tonsils out? Should you be out and about?"

Boy, am I glad that neither Dad nor Bonnie heard her comment, I thought. *It was hard enough to get out of the house.*

I was back at the reference desk with both the almanac and atlas spread open, looking up flight plans of Amelia Earhart's last journey. I found her route in the atlas. Previously I had checked in the almanac what the weather might have been like during the month of her flight. I couldn't believe the information I found!

I was finishing up my work, while Bonnie was looking over the newest fiction arrivals and Neelia was sleeping at my feet . . . when we all heard it again!

"*Mewhooooll,*" came a howl from above. Before I could stop her, Neelia raced out from under my chair, towing her leash, and leapt up the stairs to the library's attic. I was close on her tail, and Bonnie must have seen us rush by, because she followed us both up the attic stairs.

"What's going on here?!" snapped Mrs. Curtz from the bottom of the steps. "We've had enough ghost hunters here lately; we don't need a ghost-hunting cat as well. Now, back downstairs everyone."

I picked up Neelia, much to her dissatisfaction, and we marched downstairs to meet up with Mrs. Curtz. Neelia kept trying to escape my hold and run back upstairs, but I managed to hang onto her. I tried to calm her with soft whispers, but Neelia would have none of that.

"I think we best get a move on before Mrs. Curtz tears up your library card," Bonnie teased.

With the scowl we got from Mrs. Curtz on the way out the door, I wouldn't have been surprised if Mrs. Curtz went straight to the library board to petition for a "no pets" policy.

We were still home long before lunchtime, and while Bonnie again busied herself in the kitchen, I pulled out my notes and the outline Ms. Zinger had given us. In no time at all, I had the questions answered. Now it was time for me to take the outline notes and write it down so it was "interesting to the reader," as Ms. Zinger had told us.

I worked really hard on the report, and I was close to finishing up the closing paragraph. I had already planned that I would stay after school for the next day or two with Ms. Gynther in the computer lab to type my handwritten report. For years, Dad had let me type on his laptop at home. While I wasn't going to be offered a secretarial job anytime soon, it shouldn't take me too long to type out Ms. Earhart's report, making it look more official. I just hoped my little tidbit of information that I discovered would be the clincher to make my report stand out.

I couldn't wait for Frankie to get home from school so I could tell him about Neelia's actions in the library and the idea I had for us to investigate. I had a plan for the ghost, and I was basically done with Research Horror. Now, if only I could figure out who had left the footprints in the bushes.

Frankie came bounding in right at 3:10, and Neelia, bless her heart, had gone to the front window to start waiting for him at 3:00. *I wonder if she does that every school day,* I thought.

Bonnie had made a pot of stew for us for dinner during her time in the kitchen, and in addition, she baked chocolate chip cookies that were coming fresh out of the oven as Frankie walked in.

"Boy, Bonnie," Frankie bemoaned, "we're sure going to miss having you around when Ginni goes back to school tomorrow."

Bonnie just smiled as she poured all of us, including Neelia, a glass of milk—or in Neelia's case, a bowl. "I've had a great time hanging out here, I must admit," Bonnie replied. "But I'm glad that Ginni is on the mend and ready to go back to school."

When we were finished with our snack, I asked Bonnie if Frankie, Neelia, Mr. Whiskers, and I could sit outside for a bit. After assuring her that we'd leave our jackets on to not get chilled, the four of us headed for the front stoop.

"Frankie," I started, "you'll never guess what happened at the library today!"

I told him how I had convinced Dad to let Bonnie take me for a nice, calm library visit, and all was going well until the ghost started howling again. Frankie's face got pale and asked if I saw anything.

I said, "No, but you won't believe what Neelia did."

Immediately, Frankie gasped and picked Neelia up off the ground where she was chasing bugs. "Is she okay?" he cried.

"Of course, she's okay, Frankie," I said. "But Mrs. Curtz isn't going to want to see Neelia back in the library for a while." *Or ever,* I thought.

Frankie held Neelia even tighter as I told him all about her sneaking up to the attic the moment she heard the howl and her fighting me, not wanting to come back down. "But I have a plan," I added.

Frankie grinned at that. "Let's hear it," he said.

I began. "Frankie, remember when we were out petitioning, how some people were reluctant to sign the petition, and then Neelia looked at them, purred, and that almost always changed their minds and they signed?"

Frankie nodded his head. "Well, Mrs. Curtz's day off is Mondays, and I think it best if we try our plan on a day she isn't working," I said. Frankie continued to nod his head.

"On Monday after school, let's take Neelia back to the library and talk with Ms. Bellingston. She's your Sunday school teacher, right?" Again, more nods. "I bet Neelia and you can convince her to let the three of us look around the attic. I'm sure that Neelia can sniff out the ghost! How about it?"

I knew that Frankie would have to be 100% on board with the plan for it to work. Frankie had such a sweet demeanor and that, coupled with Neelia's mystifying purrs, should be enough to get us inside the attic. But Frankie himself must be convinced that it'll work as well.

Frankie held Neelia up over his head and asked her what she thought about the plan. She purred, leaned down, and licked his cheek. "I guess we're all set," Frankie laughed.

CHAPTER 8

BACK AT SCHOOL

I woke up Wednesday morning as if it were the first day back at school after summer break. I was nervous and excited. I was also pleased that I had my report done, *and* I had finished all the homework that Ms. Zinger had sent home.

When walking to the classroom, I felt like a celebrity. Everyone was excited to welcome me back, giving me hugs, then laughing, and pulling back asking if they had hugged me too tightly. I knew this popularity status was short-lived, so I just let everyone gush while I enjoyed the attention.

But my good-mood bubble was soon popped. As Ms. Zinger got our attention for the day's announcements, she reminded us that we were going to start presenting our famous person reports tomorrow! *And here I thought I was on top of things.*

"Ginni," Ms. Zinger called, "since you've been gone for so long, you can take some extra time if you need it."

With my mind racing, I thought I could get to the computer lab after school, print out a great picture of Amelia Earhart, type my one-page report, and be ready tomorrow.

"Thanks for the offer," I told Ms. Zinger, "but I'll be ready."

Ms. Zinger gave me one of her supportive smiles and started the day's reading lesson.

After school, I texted Dad to let him know I was staying late to type the report in the computer lab and had arranged for Frankie to go home with the Pebbles girls.

I couldn't believe how helpful Mrs. Gynter was in the computer lab. She sat right next to me as we searched the internet for the best picture of Amelia Earhart. She then helped me make sure that it was centered perfectly on the paper, and we put a frame around it. When I knew it was time for her to be leaving work, she told me that she'd be happy to stay longer so I could finish.

Dad was setting the table for dinner as I walked in from school. "Honey, you look exhausted! I shouldn't have let you stay late at school. Here, sit down while I get the meatloaf on the table."

"You may have been right, Dad," I conceded.

"Well, at least I've lived long enough to hear that!" Dad exclaimed with a grin.

I smirked at him and continued, "But I really wanted to be ready for my report tomorrow. Ms. Zinger said she'd give me extra time since I've been gone, but I wanted to impress her by being ready."

"Oh, honey," Dad said kindly, "you don't have to kill yourself to impress your teachers. Ms. Zinger already thinks the world of you."

"Maybe, but I told her I'd be ready, and I didn't want to disappoint myself either," I confessed.

"If you don't grow up to be a senator or an executive of a company or something, I'll be surprised." And with that, Dad came over to me and gave me one of his bear hugs.

"Or a Navy pilot," I said so softly into his chest that I knew he couldn't have heard me.

"Frankie, time for dinner!" Dad called as he left me and put all the food out on the table.

"When did you get home, Ginni?" Frankie asked as he sat on his chair and Neelia jumped up on hers.

"Just minutes ago," I told him.

"You look tired," Frankie said.

"Don't you start, too!" I pretended to scold.

After dinner, I helped Dad clear the table, and then he scooted me off to bed. I must admit, I didn't argue with him. It had been a long day.

"Ginni . . . Ginni, wake up!" Frankie whispered.

I was being rudely shaken by my shoulders as I fought to wake from a deep sleep.

"What is it?" I asked as I rubbed my eyes. Frankie was wide-eyed and standing at the head of my bed.

"There are noises outside the front of the house!" he cried. "I think the footstep kid is back. Neelia's not happy either."

I looked down and saw Neelia circling around Frankie's legs and biting his pajama bottoms as if to pull him along. I had left Mr. Whiskers in his cage last night, and he was running on his wheel as if he were being chased.

Just then we both heard the familiar swooping sound of Tyto flying close to the house.

Something indeed was going on!

I pulled on my robe and slippers and grabbed Frankie's hand as we cautiously descended the curved staircase.

"I think we should get Dad," I said to Frankie. But as soon as the words were out of my mouth, Dad, too, was pulling on his robe and coming to the front door.

"You guys must have heard the noise as well," Dad said. "Stay back in the living room while I check this out."

I didn't think it was the right time to tell Dad that it probably was an intruder wearing a child's size 10 shoe and that we didn't have much to worry about. Nevertheless, we backed up to the living room, and I grabbed Frankie's hand tighter as Dad swung the door open and turned on the outside light.

"Oh, my god!" Dad exclaimed with concern as he just stood there staring.

"What?!" we both cried out.

Dad didn't say anything but simply stepped outside and walked toward the bushes where we had seen the mystery footprints.

Neelia was mewing and Tyto was perched on the maple tree in the front yard—both of them were watching as Dad gently guided the peeper into the living room.

"Scott?!" Frankie quietly cried out as he rushed to his friend. I stood there dumbfounded.

But before Frankie could get to Scott, Dad put his arm out to stop him.

"Quiet, you two," Dad gently said. Then Dad guided Scott to the couch and helped him sit down.

"What's going on?" I whispered as soon as Scott was sitting down. He looked as if he were in a trance.

"I believe Scott is sleepwalking," Dad said. Neelia went over to Scott and laid down by his feet.

Surprisingly, she didn't jump on his lap. Neelia was always simply amazing and seemed to know exactly what people needed.

"I'm going to call Steve," Dad told us. "I don't know much about sleepwalking, but I know it's best not to severely awaken the sleepwalker. Let's see if Scott will sit comfortably on the couch until Steve can get here."

It took forever for the phone to stop ringing and Dad to start talking. I glanced at the clock, and I saw that it was 1 a.m. No wonder it took so long for Steve to answer the phone.

Dad stepped back into the living room and was relieved to see that Scott was still sitting calmly on the couch.

None of us knew what to say, so we sat a distance away from Scott so we didn't disturb him and waited the 10 minutes it took for Steve to arrive.

Dad saw Steve's car pull into the driveway, and he opened the front door to let Steve in, so Steve didn't need to knock or ring the doorbell.

"I'm so sorry," Steve began to say. "I had no idea that Scott was getting out of the house on his sleep-walking ventures. Looks like I'll be adding locks to the doors high enough so that Scott can't reach them. This isn't only embarrassing, but it's dangerous! Scott must have made his way over here in his sleep to visit Frankie. I don't have to tell you just how important their friendship has turned out to be to Scott."

"Don't think a thing about being embarrassed, Steve," Dad told him. "But, yes, Scott can't be walking around town asleep in the middle of the night. I, too, am happy that they have become good friends—it's been good for Frankie as well."

Steve said, "Let me see if I can guide him home. He usually is very compliant when he's sleepwalking. I'll stop by this weekend, and we can visit more."

I didn't know what Steve meant by "visit more," but by now I was very ready to go back to bed. As Dad was shutting the door behind Steve and Scott, I heard him say thanks to Tyto for helping alert us about Scott. *And to think this is a guy who never wanted pets!* I had to grin to myself.

CHAPTER 9

RESEARCH HORROR DELIVERED . . . ALMOST

Even after a night of interrupted sleep, I was up and anxious to get to school. Since the mystery of the footprints had been solved, I was now ready to be done with the school project that had been consuming my time and efforts. Then all that was left was the ghost.

"Boys and girls," Ms. Zinger began, "today we get to hear from many of you about your famous person. I hope you all are as excited as I am. Remember, your grade for your report will not only be based on your written work, but your presentation as well. This is your time to shine. You are the expert on the person you've chosen. Now is the time to share that expertise. Additionally, another part of your grade will be based on your being a good and polite listener for all your classmates."

When Ms. Zinger mentioned the last part about being a good listener, I could have sworn she looked directly at Stanley. Guess she knows her students pretty well.

"Now, I don't think that we'll get through all the reports today, even though we are presenting them during our reading and history class periods, so you can plan on listening to some reports tomorrow as well. To be fair, I have each of your names on a slip of paper in this little box. When I pull out your name, it's your turn to share. Let's begin."

And with that, Ms. Zinger pulled out the first slip of paper. "Heather," she said.

I silently groaned for my friend. Heather, I thought, would be too shy to be the first person to give the report. But Heather must have taken Ms. Zinger's words to heart, because she did shine while she was up front reading. You could tell she knew a great deal about Helen Keller, and she had typed two full pages on the fascinating woman.

From there, Ms. Zinger called out four more names, but none of them did as nice of a job as Heather. I was so proud of her. Then came name number six—Stanley.

Stanley swaggered to the front of the room and stood still until he had everyone's undivided attention. Boy, does he already know how to command an audience!

Stanley cleared his throat and began, "I chose my person because I have a close connection to chocolate."

As soon as he said this, he looked directly at me, and I straightened in my chair as much as possible. *Where was he going with this?*

"Last month," Stanley continued, "we almost lost our beloved chocolate shop. If it wasn't for my efforts to get thousands of signatures on a petition, Sweet Georgina's would have had to close her shop for sure. Yes, I had a little help, but I'm proud to stand behind the success of this petition. My report is on Milton S. Hershey, a famous chocolatier."

I was steaming mad. Stanley made it sound like *he* was the one who tramped all around Makawee and that everything was his idea. I looked over at Ms. Zinger and was ready to blurt out my side of the story. She calmly looked at me, nodded her head, and gave me a look that settled me back down. Her look conveyed that it was okay; we all know the true story.

Stanley ended his report by passing out a Hershey kiss to each one of us. It was everything I could do not to pick it up and throw it at him! Again, I got a calming look from Ms. Zinger, and I took a deep breath and settled down.

"Let's take a 10-minute bathroom break and then continue, boys and girls," Ms. Zinger said. As the kids were leaving their seats for break, Ms. Zinger walked by my desk and put her hand on my shoulder, telling me what her looks conveyed. "It's okay, Ginni. Stanley is simply trying to save face. The whole town knows that it was you, your brother, and your father who made things happen for Georgina. Stanley is just jealous."

"Thanks, Ms. Zinger. I guess I shouldn't go punch him in the nose then," I said with an evil grin on my face.

"That'd be best," Ms. Zinger laughed. "Now, go get a drink of water before we begin again."

My name didn't get called until that afternoon during our history class period. Now, it was my turn to go to the front of the class and read my report. I had worn my fisherman's sweater—the one Mom had knit for me— and I also carried my birthday thimble she gave me in my pocket. Wearing her sweater and carrying the thimble made me feel like she was there with her arms wrapped around me. *I believe I can do this on Amelia Earhart; I believe I can do this . . .* I kept repeating to myself.

I stood tall in the center of the classroom, cleared my throat, and began, "My report is on one of the first female pilots, Amelia Earhart."

No sooner had I gotten the words out of my mouth when Stanley blurted from his seat, "Didn't she die . . . just like your mom?"

The room instantly became silent. I froze. Out of the corner of my eye, I saw that Ms. Zinger had hung her head. My first reaction should have been to burst into tears, but for some reason, I didn't.

While I know I stood there for only a few seconds, it seemed like minutes had passed before Ms. Zinger stood up from her chair and in a calm, but firm, voice said, "Stanley, to the hall."

All the kids liked Ms. Zinger, so rarely did anyone ever misbehave in her classroom. She hardly ever needed to send anyone out to the hall. So, when she said this, I wasn't surprised to hear slight gasps from many of the kids.

Ms. Zinger came over to me, leaned down so she could look me in the eye, and quietly talked to me. "Do you want to do your report at another time?" she asked.

"No," I said, "I'll be okay." While I may have sounded confident, I'm glad Ms. Zinger couldn't feel the butterflies that were fluttering in my stomach.

She straightened up and faced the classroom before she told everyone to take a 10-minute break, and she'd be right back. "Ginni, take your seat until I get back."

I scooted back to my desk as Ms. Zinger left the classroom. No one said anything for the first minute. But then some kids started visiting, and Heather, bless her heart, came over to my desk.

"What Stanley said was just horrid!" she exclaimed. Pretty soon I had a small handful of kids surrounding my desk, all saying how mean Stanley was and asking if I was okay.

I told everyone I was fine, but to be honest, I'd rather have had them all stay at their seats. I felt like they were all watching me to see if I'd start crying or something. And I was having a tough time hanging on and not bursting into tears.

Ms. Zinger soon stepped back into the classroom, minus Stanley, and coolly announced that we were going to switch to our science lesson for the day and that we would get back to our biographies tomorrow. She questioningly looked over at me with her eyebrows raised, and I gave her a slight nod back. She nodded, and I dug out my science book—all the while wondering where Stanley was.

The school day finished, and Stanley never did come back to class. I didn't know what to make of that, and I was nervous about the next time I'd see him.

The Pebbles girls were all talking about his comment, and they were so mad at Stanley during our walk home. Apparently, it didn't take long for the news to spread throughout the school. All three girls gave me a great big hug when we split to go to our homes.

"I suppose I had better tell Dad," I commented to Frankie. "I wouldn't be surprised if the news didn't get to the downtown businesses as well as throughout the school."

Frankie nodded. From meeting up with him in the school yard and all during our walk home, Frankie said nothing. He had given me a great, supportive hug as soon as he saw me, and that was better than any words he could have said.

While Tyto often flies overhead on our way home, today it seemed he flew closer and was more protective.

I didn't have long to wait to tell Dad, because he opened the front door for us as we were walking up the sidewalk.

That was it. I had held it together all this time, but seeing Dad's anguished face at the front door, knowing he came home from work early to be by my side, was more than I could take. I burst out crying as I ran into his arms.

"My sweet little girl," Dad said to comfort me, as he held me in his arms.

It took a bit, but after a while, I calmed down and the three of us went into the kitchen. Dad had placed Mr. Whiskers in a box, waiting for me. I picked him up, and with Neelia on my lap, Mr. Whiskers nuzzled on my shoulder, Tyto at the window, and Dad and Frankie sitting at the table next to me, I was surrounded by the entire Pearl family. For a few minutes, we all just sat there.

Finally, Dad asked, "What was Ms. Zinger's response to the situation?"

"Well," I began, "she immediately sent Stanley to the hall and stepped out of the room for about ten minutes. Stanley never came back."

Just then, Dad's phone rang, and he went to his home office to answer it.

"Ginni, that was Ms. Zinger," Dad said, coming back to the kitchen. "You need to know that she has set up a meeting with you and Stanley and his dad tomorrow morning before school. I'll be there as well."

A few tears trickled down as I said, "Dad, can't we just forget it happened? I really don't want to confront Stanley."

"It'll be okay, honey," Dad said. "None of us at the table are going to let anything happen that doesn't support you. Plus, Stanley needs to understand that he really crossed the line this time. This went way beyond just being a mean kid comment."

"Come on, let's go to the Village Diner for dinner tonight. I don't feel like cooking," Dad said, trying to lighten the mood. "Burgers and chicken nuggets on me!"

I thought about going upstairs to change out of my school clothes, but I changed my mind. If ever I needed to feel Mom close to me, it was now, and I wanted to be wearing her sweater. I'd just have to be super careful not to spill ketchup on it!

Chelsea, our favorite waitress, immediately came to our table with our drinks already poured. It was so cool when she did that, but I could swear she, too, had heard the news, because it seemed like she had a very sympathetic look on her face. *I must be paranoid,* I thought. *Just enjoy the burger.*

When we got home from dinner, Dad turned on a movie, went to make popcorn, and even brought out cups of his famous hot cocoa. Boy, was he turning on the "feel good" charm. But I must admit, his loving actions helped to fill my heart and push away all the anger and hatred I was feeling toward Stanley. I was able to settle down and enjoy the movie while nibbling the popcorn and sipping hot cocoa. Of course, having Neelia curled up on my lap and Mr. Whiskers on my shoulder with Tyto peering in from the window, all helped as well.

CHAPTER 10

THE APOLOGY

Boy, was I dreading this morning. I truly did not want to have a big meeting on yesterday's incident. I simply wanted to move forward. It wasn't like Stanley was going to change being who he was. But I didn't get a say in the matter. And wasn't I being punished as well, having to be at school 45 minutes early?

But there I was, sitting at a big conference table, in a room off Ms. Nineon's office. Ms. Nineon is our principal, and while I've never been in trouble before that had landed me in her office, I didn't want to start now—even though I was on the "good" side.

Dad and I arrived there first, but it wasn't long before Stanley and his dad came walking in. I must admit that Stanley wasn't walking with his normal cocky walk. *Good,* I thought.

Ms. Nineon and Ms. Zinger followed Stanley in, and we began.

"I heard what was said in Ms. Zinger's class yesterday," Ms. Nineon said, "and I must say that I'm appalled that any of our students here at Makawee Elementary would say such a cruel thing. I want you all to know that we believe building good character is just as important as building good academics. You can be as smart as a whip, but if you are an unkind, uncaring person, you are not going to go very far in this life."

During Ms. Nineon's speech, Stanley was looking hard at the table.

Ms. Zinger chimed in as well, "Stanley, I, too, must admit that I was utterly taken back by what you said to Ginni yesterday. We all know you like to tease, and that many times you push the boundaries, but I never would have expected such a comment from any of my students, even you."

I was a little surprised when I looked at Stanley after Ms. Zinger spoke to him. He actually looked embarrassed. Could it be that he was upset with himself, that he had disappointed Ms. Zinger? I know I would have been.

Ms. Nineon took over again, "Now that you know how you disappointed all of us at this table, it's time for us to move on—especially for Ginni's sake. Mr. McMann, you mentioned you had some thoughts when I talked to you earlier on the phone."

"Yes, Ms. Nineon," said Stanley's dad. "Let me begin by apologizing for my son. There can be no excuse for his comment, and I agree with all of you—this goes far beyond being a silly kid thing. I feel guilty that both Stanley's mom and I have demanding careers and that we must work long hours. That's on us, and we'll have to see if we can make adjustments in order to provide more support for our wayward son."

Wayward son, I thought. *Wow, this was serious.*

"Mr. McMann and I have talked about a school consequence," said Ms. Nineon, "and have come to a good agreement. Stanley will stay in from recess for as long as it takes in order to complete biography reports on two people who are known for outstanding character. Once those reports are complete, Stanley will read them aloud to the class."

This was the first time that Stanley raised his head. I could tell he was surprised. "*Two* reports?" he asked incredulously. "*And* read them aloud to the class!"

Ms. Zinger answered Stanley, "Yes, Stanley, two reports, and I think the first one should be on Mother Teresa. She was a remarkable woman."

"But isn't she a nun or something?" Stanley asked. "We can't do church stuff here at school."

"I thought about that, Stanley," Ms. Zinger said, "and I did a little research. Mother Teresa was much more than a religious figure. And I quote, 'She was one of the highest examples of service to our humanity.' You will not be researching her religious beliefs, but her humanitarian efforts and all she did to help those in need. We'll work on the second person together once you are done with the Mother Teresa report.

"And as to reading the reports aloud to the class, Stanley, you offended many of the students in the room. They, too, need to know you regret your comment. Speaking of, I believe it is time for your apology to Ginni."

Stanley started talking, but his father nudged him and told him he had to look at me for the apology. I truly would have liked Stanley to continue to apologize to the table, but I gathered my strength and looked him in the eye.

"I'm sorry, Ginni," Stanley said. "I really don't know what came over me. I can't imagine how I'd feel if it were my mother who died last summer. Sometimes things come out of my mouth before I even think."

Someone had helped him with that apology, that's for sure, I thought. "Maybe you should slow down your mouth, then," I said.

That brought a smile from everyone at the table, including Stanley.

Mr. McMann piped up, "I feel comfortable that we have the school issue taken care of the best that we can, but I also want Stanley to make amends at home. Jim, what chores does Ginni do around the house that can become Stanley's responsibility for the next month?"

Stanley again raised his head from looking at the table. He didn't expect this either.

"Well, let's see," said Dad. "Ginni's job is to take the garbage to the curb every week, and she helps set and clear the table for dinner. I was also going to ask for her help in cleaning out the garage one of the first nice Saturdays we have."

"Perfect. Stanley will be over every week for the next month to wheel out the garbage, and as for dinner, just text me when you're done eating, and I'll send Stanley right over to clear the table—even if he's not done with his own dinner," said Mr. McMann.

"Ginni," Dad said, "you have a month reprieve, *and* you get out of cleaning the garage!"

I smiled at Dad, and I hope he didn't realize that I had forced the smile. Truth be told, I'd rather continue doing my own chores and keep Stanley away, but I know everyone was trying to make me feel compensated. Didn't they know that nothing could take away the hurt that Stanley caused me when I was standing in front of the class? But I guess this would be the steps we'd take to move on.

When we were done with the meeting, there was just enough time to get to class, which was a good thing. I really didn't want to stand around trying to explain to everyone what had happened. Ms. Zinger, my savior, rescued me from the endless questioning from the other kids by starting out the class and updating everyone on what had happened. She gave an abbreviated version, but the class knew Stanley would be presenting two reports on people with good character. She also asked if Stanley had anything to say.

Surprisingly, Stanley stood up and said, "I'm sorry, everyone, for disrupting class. And I'm sorry to Ginni. I shouldn't have said what I did."

There were looks all around as Stanley made his apology. To be honest, he even looked serious when he talked. I wasn't the only one amazed.

Thankfully, Ms. Zinger went straight to our reading lesson, saying that we'd save the last of the biography reports for the afternoon.

At recess, I updated Catherine and her sisters on how things went in the morning. I got hugs all around, and we all agreed that we'd enjoy this "kinder" Stanley for as long as it lasted.

Then it was time for the last three biography reports. I couldn't wear my fisherman's sweater again, so instead

I wore a shirt that Mom had helped me embroider. It was just a t-shirt and a little cool for the season, but I had to have something that was part of her. And, of course, the thimble was still in my pocket.

When I was called, I went to the front of the room, cleared my throat, and again announced that my report was on Amelia Earhart. As soon as I said those words, I looked directly at Stanley—but he had his head down, thoroughly staring at the top of his desk, and didn't meet my eye.

I took a second after I introduced my report, told myself I believed I could do this, and began. I had really fallen in love with this pioneering woman, and it wasn't hard to share my excitement about all that I had found out. I hoped I "shined." Before long, there it was—the conclusion.

"To conclude, I found an interesting and sad fact regarding Ms. Earhart. She was advised to never smile showing her teeth in professional photographs because she had a gap between her two front teeth. And indeed, if you do a Google image search, you will find that in most of her photographs, Ms. Earhart is smiling with her mouth closed. With all she accomplished, it's too bad she had to worry about something silly like a gap between her teeth."

I gave a little bow and started heading back to my desk. And then I was completely blown away because up popped Heather, giving me a standing ovation. In a matter of seconds, the rest of the class stood up and started clapping. I just stood there with my mouth open and tears in my eyes. Even Ms. Zinger stood up and politely clapped. When I looked toward Stanley, I saw that he was standing but not clapping. But he did look at me with a sideways smirk on his face. It was almost like he, too, was proud of me.

I walked to my desk and put my hand in my pocket to hang onto the thimble. *I guess the believing helped,* I thought.

When Frankie and I got home, we changed our clothes, grabbed Neelia, and with Tyto in flight, we went for a walk. Being cooped up in the house for so many days, it felt good to walk outside. "How about heading to Totem Trails Park?" I asked.

Frankie nodded, and we were off. We wouldn't have much time today to enjoy the nature trails or the curly slide, but just getting out was enough for me.

When we got home, Dad had made one of my favorite dinners—his famous spaghetti and buttery garlic toast. Talk about comfort food!

It was very odd having Stanley come over after dinner to help Dad clear the table, but I didn't stick around and went up to my room. Stanley was gone before too long. Since it was Friday night, the three of us decided to play a game of Monopoly. Dad usually wins hands-down at this game, but this time, I came out with all the money. I think Dad let me win, but who cares. What mattered was we were all there. Mr. Whiskers was asleep on my lap, and Neelia was on Frankie's, while Tyto "hooted" occasionally, to remind us he was there, too, watching from the window.

Saturday morning, as promised, Steve stopped over to talk with Dad. After I greeted him and let him into the house, Dad stepped out of his home office, and the two of them went back inside to talk. I was surprised that Steve was in Dad's office for almost an hour. It wasn't as though I was hanging around trying to listen in, but I'll admit, I didn't go too far away, either.

When the office door opened, Steve had a sad look on his face, but he stopped by to give me a hug before he left. "I heard you had a hard week too, Ginni," he said. "I'm glad you stood up for yourself!"

I didn't know how I had stood up for myself. It was more like Ms. Zinger and Ms. Nineon stood up for me, but I didn't argue. I just hugged him back and told him thanks.

"Ginni, go get your brother, and we'll have a talk," Dad said as soon as Steve left.

I yelled up the staircase, "Frankie!" and he came right down, sitting on the stairs with Neelia on his lap, going bumpity-bump down the stairs. I had to giggle at this familiar game they had.

We went right into Dad's office as soon as Frankie had landed, and Dad told us both to sit.

"As you know, Steve was just here, and he wanted us to know a little of Scott's background. I told him that we were indeed curious since it was a bit unusual for a grandchild to be visiting this long, but that it really was none of our business. Steve went on to say that we had been so good to them, especially you, Frankie, and he thought it best for us to know the story."

Frankie smiled when he was complimented, and I could tell he was pleased. "I'm not just being nice to Scott to be good, Dad. Scott's a cool kid."

"I'm glad you think that, Frankie, but you have gone out of your way to make him feel at home here in Makawee and Steve appreciates that," Dad said.

Again, Frankie smiled.

"Anyway," Dad continued, "what I'm going to tell you can go no further than this office. No telling the Pebbles girls, no school mates, and not even teachers. Steve is taking us into his confidence so that we, all together, can support Scott. But you must understand, you can talk to no one about this except for me and Steve. Steve bringing us into this family issue is a huge honor and obligation, and one we will not fail. Do I have a promise from both of you that Scott's story stays only among us?"

I had never seen Dad so serious. "Of course," I said.

"Frankie?" Dad asked.

"Yes, Dad," Frankie said, "whatever we can do to help Scott."

"Well, as we've talked about before, it is unusual for Scott to be living here with his grandfather. Here's what happened . . . About a year ago, Scott's parents got in a car accident, and while not paralyzed or anything, they both were seriously hurt. They were given pain medication during the healing process. Several months later, their bodies had basically healed, but what happened is that both of his parents had gotten addicted to the pain medication. This has become a serious problem, and there's no easy answer. On one hand, you need the pain relief so that you can heal and not lie in bed suffering, but on the other hand, too often the patient gets so addicted to pain medication that they feel they can't go on without it.

Both of his parents were seriously addicted, so much so that the court ordered that they go to a special hospital to help them get off the pain medication. Of course, that meant that Scott needed a place to live. Steve was only too happy to not only help, but to be able to spend more time with Scott, who he dearly loves."

After that explanation, neither of us had anything to say. Finally, I broke the silence and said, "Wow! No wonder Scott seems sad so often. Imagine what he must have gone through before his parents got help. Dad, you can count on us. Neither of us will breathe a word of his story to anyone, and we both will continue to make Scott feel at home here in Makawee."

Dad smiled at me and looked at Frankie who nodded with a wide-eyed look on his face. *Pretty heavy stuff for a first grader*, I thought. But Scott was closest to Frankie, so he had to know.

"I feel pretty special that Steve trusts us, Dad. I knew he'd feel comfortable sharing with you, but it's neat that he trusts us, too," I said.

"You've earned that trust, both of you," Dad said. And then he came out from behind his desk, and we all three hugged.

CHAPTER 11

GHOST FOUND

The weekend was calm. Stanley kept coming over to clear the table, and he and Dad made plans to clean out the garage next Saturday if the weather was decent. I was getting used to having a "butler" clear the table. My only regret was that it wasn't the dead of winter when Stanley had to take the garbage to the curb. Fighting the snow, cold, and ice was always a pain during the winter months, but taking the garbage out in March was no big deal. Oh, well.

On Sunday night, Frankie and I had a meeting in my bedroom to finalize the ghost-hunting plans. If all went as we hoped, I was pretty sure that Neelia would solve this mystery just like she solved the culprit mystery of who was stealing small objects during Christmas break.

While I wanted to race home with Frankie right after school on Monday, I thought it best to act as normal as possible. We hadn't brought the Pebbles girls into this mystery, and it was too late to do so now. Frankie had wanted to ask Scott to go along with us as well, but I told him we'd have a much better chance convincing Ms. Bellingston to let just the three of us up in the attic than to bring along additional kids. Frankie had to admit that I was probably right.

So, we dropped off the Pebbles, and hurried home to change clothes and grab Neelia. It seemed like she knew something special was about to happen because she pranced around while Frankie tried to get her leash hooked.

"Hold still, little girl," Frankie laughed as Neelia circled.

As Frankie was harnessing Neelia, I had an idea. "Hang on a minute, Frankie. I'll be right back down."

I went up to my bedroom and went to Mr. Whiskers' cage. "Hey, little guy, what do you think about a trip to the library?" At that, Mr. Whiskers started circling just as Neelia had.

"Okay, okay," I laughed. "But you must stay hidden. The librarians would have my hide if they knew I brought a mouse into the library! Even though it's warm, I'll wear my scarf with the pocket that you rode in when we were petitioning, okay?"

In a jiffy, I was back downstairs, and Frankie had managed to get Neelia's harness on.

"Ginni, it's not cold out. Why did you go upstairs to get your scarf? Does your throat hurt?" Frankie asked with concern.

And then Mr. Whiskers peeked his head out, and Frankie laughed out loud.

Tyto followed us to the library. When we got to the front steps, I looked at Frankie and said, "You know the plan. Just be cool. Act your innocent self and let Neelia do her magic. Got it?"

Frankie swallowed hard and nodded. As soon as we got to the top of the steps, Frankie reached down and picked up Neelia. I opened the huge door, and we walked in.

We were in luck! There were no customers at the desk, and Ms. Bellingston was looking intently at something on the computer. Not a patron in sight.

Frankie, carrying Neelia, walked right up to the desk and politely said, "Excuse me, Ms. Bellingston. May I ask you a question?"

Ms. Bellingston looked away from her screen, and it took a second for her to realize that it was Frankie in front of her. "Why, it's you, Frankie! Of course, you may ask me a question. How can I help you?"

Right then, Neelia went into high gear. She purred like I never heard from her before, and the loving look in her eyes when she gazed at Ms. Bellingston was usually only used for Frankie. Ms. Bellingston couldn't help but reach across the desk and start petting Neelia.

"Well," Frankie began, "my sister was here the other day working on her report when she heard the ghost in the attic. Neelia, that's our kitten here, got very excited. We think that if you let the three of us in the attic that Neelia might be able to find the ghost."

"Really . . . " Ms. Bellingston trailed off. "A ghost in the attic you say . . . "

Boy, Neelia really had Ms. Bellingston mesmerized. Finally, she nodded her head and said, "Of course, why not? What harm could it do?"

And with that, she got a special key out from the desk drawer and walked us upstairs.

"Thank you," Frankie said. "I'm sure we won't be long."

I looked at Frankie and Neelia as we reached the landing, and they both were grinning like fools. I had to laugh that our plan had worked so easily.

Ms. Bellingston opened the attic door and said, "I can't stay with you two—I'm the only one here right now—so I must get back to the desk. Promise me you won't mess anything up."

"We promise," we said in unison as Neelia wriggled frantically to get down.

Just as soon as Neelia started prowling, Mr. Whiskers jumped from my scarf, and both he and Neelia were madly sniffing the attic floor.

I wasn't sure I liked Mr. Whiskers running around free like that. It's easy for a small mouse to get himself into trouble, but he seemed to know what he was doing.

Suddenly, there was a huge *bang* from the far corner of the attic, followed by thumps and bumps. Frankie and I almost jumped out of our skins. The bang was 10 times louder up here than what we had been hearing downstairs.

In a matter of seconds, we heard Ms. Bellingston calling from downstairs asking if we were alright.

"We're just fine up here!" I managed to call out now that my heart had stopped racing. "I think Neelia is on to something. Just go back to the desk. We'll be fine." I sure sounded more confident than I felt. Out of the corner of my eye, I saw a movement outside the window. There was Tyto circling.

Right then, Mr. Whiskers went crazy. He darted this way and that, acting like a wild animal was chasing him. And squeak! I had never heard him squeak so loudly before.

And then I thought, *Since no critter is chasing him, maybe he's tempting someone to come and get him, like in dodgeball. Or a mouse game of 'Ha, ha, ha, you can't catch me.'*

When I realized this, I got very, very scared. What if he was tempting something? And what if he got caught? But then I saw Neelia circling around Mr. Whiskers, almost like she was guarding him. *They're working like a team,* I thought, *trying to lure out the ghost!*

There was another loud *clunk,* and what then came sneaking out from the far dark corner? A small little tabby cat! But something wasn't right. The cat was walking funny.

Frankie got down on his knees and softly started cooing to the cat, and Neelia positioned herself behind the tabby so it couldn't sneak away.

As soon as the cat realized that it was trapped, it forgot all about trying to chase Mr. Whiskers and instead went running wildly around the entire attic. The cat was tripping over chairs that had been placed up there for storage, bouncing off tables and countertops, and making a ruckus like I had never heard before.

When the cat was running around, I finally got a good look at why it was walking funny. The cat had a small metal tub stuck on his foot!

But all the ruckus caused Ms. Bellingston to not only call from the bottom of the stairs, but to climb up to the attic to check on us.

"My goodness!" she exclaimed. "What is going on up here?"

Just as she called that out, I leapt in front of the cat who was trying to jump past me to get back to his corner. Somehow, I managed to catch him in mid-flight. I hung on tightly and started to say soothing words into his little ear.

Ms. Bellingston wasn't the only one who ventured upstairs. It seemed everyone who was in the library also made the trip to the attic. As soon as she saw the terrified cat, she immediately scooted everyone downstairs.

"Are you okay, Ginni?" she asked. "It didn't bite you, did it?"

"No, I'm okay," I answered as the cat was still trying to get away.

"Let me run downstairs and call Dr. Little from the Little Paws Veterinarian Clinic. I'll ask him to send someone over with a cat carrier, and we'll have this little guy checked out," said Ms. Bellingston.

It was then that she noticed that the cat had a tub stuck on his foot.

"What on earth happened here?" she exclaimed. "Why, that's our small library glue tub. How did that get stuck on his foot?"

By now, Frankie, carrying Neelia while Mr. Whiskers was hidden in his pocket, came over to the cat. It was amazing the calming effect that both Frankie and Neelia had over the frightened kitty. By the time the vet tech came with the carrier, the cat was much calmer and went with the tech without any problem.

"What have we here?" demanded Mrs. Curtz as all of us marched down the stairs.

Oh boy, I thought, *we're toast now.*

The vet tech took over, thankfully, and opened the carrier to show Mrs. Curtz what had been making such a fuss in the attic.

"With his foot caught in library glue, poor thing," said Mrs. Curtz, reaching inside to pet the cat. I didn't understand the look, but Ms. Bellingston had a very shocked expression on her face while Mrs. Curtz was petting the scared cat.

"I'm very glad Ms. Bellingston called me to tell me the ghost was caught. I came right over. Take good care of this precious little thing," Mrs. Curtz said, "and call me the minute it's ready to be picked up from the clinic."

Mrs. Curtz came over to us, and I thought we were going to get chewed out for sure. But instead, she dropped to her knees and pulled us in for a hug.

"Thank you, my dears," she said. "And I'm sorry that I've not been very kind to Neelia when she's visited the library. I'm afraid I've been a bit jealous, you see. My very special kitty that I had for nineteen years died a year ago this month, and every time I saw Neelia, I felt the pain of her loss.

"What you have done is not only solve the mystery of our ghost, but you also saved a life. That poor creature couldn't have lasted much longer stuck in the attic. It must have been catching mice to eat. Although with the metal tub stuck on its foot, it had to be difficult indeed."

When she said this, I saw the bulge in Frankie's pocket wiggle. I knew Mr. Whiskers was either getting tired of being cramped in a pocket, or he didn't like the comment about eating mice. I shook my head as I laughed at myself. *Mr. Whiskers can't understand speech. Silly me!*

On Wednesday, the paper carried a front-page article announcing the ghost mystery solved. There was a picture of the cat and Mrs. Curtz after he—the reporter said it was a male cat— had been cleaned up and the tub had very carefully been removed from his paw.

Mrs. Curtz invited the entire town to stop by the library and enter their vote for a cat-naming contest. The winner would be announced the following Wednesday at a special Open House, welcoming the new library cat.

"Isn't that nice?" Dad commented while reading the paper aloud to us. "The library is going to have its own cat. Seems everyone's getting into pets these days." And with that, he gave me a great big wink.

I laughed, but then I had to finally come clean. "Dad, I have to admit something."

Dad raised his eyebrow.

"When Frankie and I went to the library to take Neelia to look in the attic, we took Mr. Whiskers along with us," I confessed.

"Let me get this right," Dad said with both his eyebrows now raised, "you took a mouse into the library. The same library where you know the librarian is already concerned about a cat?"

I hung my head a bit lower and simply nodded. "It seemed like the right thing to do, and Mr. Whiskers really wanted to go along."

"I'm not even going to ask, Ginni, about how you think your pet mouse 'wanted' to go along. Anyway, continue," Dad said.

Whew! That was the hard part. Next it was easy to share with Dad on how both Neelia and Mr. Whiskers worked together to lure the library cat from his hiding place to where I could catch him before he escaped back into the dark recesses of the attic.

Dad looked at me skeptically when I told him about Mr. Whiskers playing "catch me if you can" with the library cat. "I think you're lucky that the cat had that glue tub stuck on his foot or you could have easily been minus one pet," Dad said seriously.

"I know it was risky," I admitted, "but I was sure Neelia would take care of Mr. Whiskers."

"You're probably right," Dad said. "I'm just happy everything worked out the way it did. I'm assuming that Mrs. Curtz doesn't know about Mr. Whiskers?"

I shook my head no.

"Well, normally, I'd have you go to Mrs. Curtz and apologize to her for bringing in a mouse to the library, but since everything worked out, and Mrs. Curtz seems in love with her new library cat, I think it best we just let this be our little secret. Along with Frankie, Neelia, and Tyto," Dad added with a grin.

"Thanks, Dad," I said. "Oh, I almost forgot! I have something else to share with you." And with a big grin, I handed Dad my Amelia Earhart report that Ms. Zinger had returned to me.

OPEN HOUSE

CHAPTER 12

PARTY!

The following week was back to normal. I was still feeling 100%, schoolwork was routine, and Stanley had even finished his two biographies. His second biography coincidently was on Andrew Carnegie. We all learned that Mr. Carnegie was a business tycoon in the late 1800s and early-1900s. He was noted for providing grants for small communities to build libraries. Makawee's library was built in 1900, and it was part of the Carnegie library grant system. With all that had happened at the library these past couple of days, Ms. Zinger couldn't have found a better research project for Stanley.

But now it was Wednesday and time to attend the Open House at the library and to find out what the library cat's name was going to be.

Mrs. Curtz must have hired Sweet Georgina to provide the treats, because there were small tables of punch and her delicious chocolates spread around. Dad closed his office early, and his entire dental staff met Frankie, Neelia, and me just as we were walking up the library steps.

We got there in time to overhear Mrs. Curtz telling our local newspaper reporter the background story of the new cat, who had evidently bonded very well with Mrs. Curtz. The cat never left her arms, and he and Mrs. Curtz acted like they had been best friends forever.

"Well, I'm happy to report that due to the efforts of two of our main patrons, this little kitty has a new lease on life," we heard Mrs. Curtz say. "After things calmed down, our custodian, Jim Prew, went back up to the attic to have a look around. It seems like the lid to our library glue tub hadn't been latched correctly, so when the cat knocked it over and stepped in it, his foot got permanently caught in the fast-acting paste.

"He also found the remains of several poor little mice that had been the cat's food source strewn about. And since the work sink up there has always had a leaky faucet, this little guy had access to water as well—you can see kitty paw prints all around the sink. But I dare say, I don't know how much longer he could have existed like that. I'm just so happy that he has moved in downstairs. Everyone loves him, and he even enjoys listening to our children's story hour."

The reporter smiled at that. "And what is the cat's name?"

"Oh, we are just about to reveal that. Hang on and you'll see," Mrs. Curtz said.

When she was finished talking, Frankie spotted Scott and went off to chat with him. I was pleased that during this past week the two boys had gotten together even more frequently. Their friendship was doing them both good.

Dad went to talk with Irving while we waited for the naming ceremony, and I overheard Dad asking if he had gotten a new transmission for the Chrysler out of Mr. Smiley.

"Yep," Irving reported. "He was true to his word, although I think it pained him a bit." Both men laughed at that.

In the back corner stood the Pebbles girls, and Heather had joined them. *Good,* I thought, *she needs more friends.* I went over to chat, and I was retelling them the story of how Neelia had kept the library cat from sneaking back into her hiding place when Mrs. Curtz rang a little bell and the room fell silent.

"Thank you for attending our little Open House," Mrs. Curtz began. "I can't tell you how happy I and the entire library staff are to have you all present for our naming ceremony. But I'd like to begin by giving special thanks to someone very important. For as I've heard the story told, if it wasn't for her, this little cat of ours would probably still be our upstairs ghost."

Everyone laughed at that, but I had dreaded that she was going to call attention to me since I got us upstairs to search. From the chocolate shop petition, to being singled out from Stanley's hurtful comment, I had had enough attention for a good, long time.

So, I was very pleased when Mrs. Curtz asked for Frankie to bring Neelia up front. Frankie doesn't like attention either, but when he's holding Neelia, he doesn't mind because he knows everyone is paying attention to our sweet little kitten.

Frankie went up to stand by Mrs. Curtz who reached down and hugged them both. While she did this, the two cats meowed at each other and rubbed noses during the hug. Everyone in the room went, "Awww."

I thought of Mom and how proud she would have been about Frankie helping save the cat. I sure wish she could have been here.

Mrs. Curtz straightened up after the hug and told the story of how Neelia coaxed the library cat out from her hiding place so that he could be rescued. *Good thing Mr. Whiskers is the Pearl family's little secret,* I thought.

"Because of her insistence to find the ghost and her ingenuity, I am proud to announce that Neelia is now the first cat in Makawee's Public Library history to have her own library card!"

The reporter came up with his camera and flashed many pictures as Mrs. Curtz held the library card up in front of Neelia. Frankie just beamed, and I had a few tears running down my cheeks. I looked over at Dad, and I could tell that he, too, was very touched.

"Neelia is welcome to come to the library anytime, and I know our library cat will enjoy her visits," Mrs. Curtz concluded. And with that, she gave Frankie and Neelia another hug, and Frankie left to once again stand by Scott.

"So . . . what is going to be the name of this very special library cat?" Mrs. Curtz continued. She reached over to a large sign that had been lying face down on top of the circulation desk. Before I reveal the name that's on this sign, however, I'd like to call up the very creative person who thought of this ingenious name for our library cat."

We all were curious as to who this creative person could be. I didn't think my suggestion of Casper would

win. I didn't think that Mrs. Curtz really wanted to per-
petuate the ghost thing.

"Stanley McMann, would you please come forward?" Mrs. Curtz announced.

We all gasped. *Stanley?* I thought. *Creative?*

But up marched Stanley with his father standing proudly off in the corner.

"Stanley, without sharing the name just yet, can you tell us what made you think of such an appropriate name for our new little cat?" Mrs. Curtz asked.

"I dunno," Stanley said. "But after I had the idea for Frankie to take Neelia to go search in the library, the name came to me. I was thinking of all sorts of library words we had learned from Ms. Gynther, and I liked this one."

I smacked my head as Stanley claimed he thought of sending Neelia to the attic. *Is he ever going to learn?* I asked myself.

"Well," said Mrs. Curtz, "let me proudly introduce everyone to our new library cat named . . . Stanley, why don't you have the honor." And Mrs. Curtz handed the cat over to Stanley so she could hold up the sign for all to see. Stanley didn't look comfortable holding the cat, but at least the cat stayed in his arms.

As soon as Mrs. Curtz turned the sign around, Stanley shouted out, "Dewey! The library cat's name is Dewey."

We all laughed and applauded. Even I had to join in the fun. Ms. Gynther had been working with us diligently this entire year, helping us understand the Dewey Decimal System used for organizing nonfiction books, and it was indeed a perfect name for the new library cat.

After we milled around for 20 minutes or so, it was time to leave. Dad gathered Frankie and me, and we said our good-byes to our friends. I even looked over at Stanley and gave him a thumbs-up sign. And if I'm not mistaken, I think he blushed a bit.

We had just gotten to the bottom of the steps when we heard Mrs. Curtz call out, "Hey, you guys! I just want to say good-night and to thank you all once again for solving the ghost mystery." She said this all the while holding Dewey and waving his paw good-bye at us.

Dad waved back, and Frankie, carrying Neelia, waved her paw. Dad responded, "Don't thank us! Neelia is the one who solved the mystery. And to be the first cat in Makawee's Public Library history to have her own library card is all the thanks she needs."

Dad and Frankie started to head toward home, and Mrs. Curtz turned to walk back into the library. Right then, my eyes caught a glimpse of something very strange in the attic window.

I looked closely for several long seconds, and I swear I saw an eerie shape float back and forth in front of the window. "Look!" I cried out to Dad and Frankie.

But as soon as they turned around, the ghostly image was gone.

"What?" Dad asked.

I didn't want to explain what I thought I saw, so I lamely said, "Mrs. Curtz is still holding Dewey."

Dad looked quizzically at me, but didn't say any-thing, and turned to walk toward home.

Neelia, however, looking directly in my eyes, nodded her head, and meowed.

PUBLIC LIBRARY

COMING UP

Be sure to follow Ginni, Frankie, Neelia, Tyto, and Mr. Whiskers on their next adventure, *The Kitten Who Was Stolen*

It couldn't be worse…Neelia is stolen. Who would do such a thing?

The entire Pearl family is devastated when a fun Spring Carnival turns into a nightmare. Mr. Pearl and Ginni are obviously heartbroken with Neelia missing, but Frankie may never recover from the grief if Neelia is gone for good. Neelia, his savior who helped him heal from his mother's death, touched his heart, and saved Frankie from despair. Now Frankie is again facing overwhelming sorrow.

What Frankie doesn't know is that the entire town has gotten to know and fall in love with the darling black kitten. While Neelia isn't able to help solve this mystery, perhaps the town folks and even Tyto and Mr. Whiskers can work together to bring Neelia home.

It has to work…

ACKNOWLEDGMENTS

Vine Street Mysteries wouldn't be where it is today without the immense help from my author assistant. Without her support, encouragement, knowledge, and dedication, this series would be sorely lacking.

My team at Dartfrog must also be noted for their support in the mechanics of the publishing world. Thank you for your expertise in helping me get my stories out and shared to the world.

ABOUT THE AUTHOR

Nova DuBois has spent her life among children's books and elementary-aged children. She began her love of children's literature in her early teens when volunteering at her hometown's library where she held Saturday morning storytelling hour and assisted in maintaining the children's book area. This passion resulted in pre and post-graduate degrees in library science. She enjoys bringing stories to life for children and watching their imaginations soar.

She has her own special black cat who helps provide inspiration for the *Vine Street Mysteries* series. This is the third book of this series, and who knows where her black cat will lead her?